"Oughtn't you be making a move?"

Eleanor asked the question nervously. She didn't really like the idea of his going.

Gil's eyes burned almost auburn, dark beneath his shadowed brows. "Yes...."

And, while her heart thudded in mortified recognition of his deliberate misinterpretation of her words, he got to his feet and came to stand behind her. His fingers came to rest lightly on her shoulders, then began massaging her neck very gently.

"I didn't mean that sort of move," she said, but the words were a muffled whisper as desire caught in her throat.

"I know...."

Jenny Cartwright was born and raised in Wales. After three years at university in Kent and a year spent in the United States, she returned to Wales where she now lives. Happily married with three young children—a girl and two boys—she began to indulge her lifelong desire to write when her lively twins were very small. The peaceful solitude she enjoys while creating her romances contrasts happily with the often hectic bustle of her busy household.

STORM
OF PASSION
Jenny Cartwright

Harlequin Books

TORONTO • NEW YORK • LONDON
AMSTERDAM • PARIS • SYDNEY • HAMBURG
STOCKHOLM • ATHENS • TOKYO • MILAN
MADRID • WARSAW • BUDAPEST • AUCKLAND

ISBN 0-373-17168-4

STORM OF PASSION

CHAPTER ONE

THE man was looking intently at her face. 'Your lips are a sort of greenish white, with a blue line around them,' he said severely.

'I don't care!' exclaimed Eleanor. 'I'm perfectly all right, I tell you.'

'If you keep on saying that I'll send you to hospital with suspected brain damage. I've never seen anyone less all right in all my life.'

Eleanor teetered to her feet, trying to look the picture of health. She raised a numb hand to her head to try and claw some of the drenched strands of long, dark hair away from her eyes. 'Look,' she said stolidly. 'I'm fine. See!' and she took a couple of shaky steps to prove her point. It was the sand that was at fault. It slithered about a bit under her feet. If it hadn't been for the sand she wouldn't have sat down again with such a thump.

'There!' said the man, triumphantly. 'That proves it. You can't even walk. You're in shock, my girl, and all you can do is give in gracefully and wait for it to pass.'

'You stop being so nasty to the girl!' came a voice from the gaggle of people who had clustered around her. 'She's a heroine!' and a large woman of uncertain age pushed forward and laid a protective arm around Eleanor's naked shoulders.

There was a muttering of agreement from the little crowd.

'She deserves a medal!' came one voice, and then

another called, 'She risked her life trying to save that little boy. You lay off her!'

'Huh!' exploded the harsh voice of the man. 'She risked my life, saving them both, if you want the truth. She was an idiot. Pure and simple.'

'Leave me alone!' cried Eleanor. 'I'm all right and the child is all right, and surely that's all that matters?'

In response the man dropped a tartan rug over her trembling shoulders, scooped her up in his arms, and marched up the beach with her. Oddly, the sand didn't seem to have any effect beneath his bare feet, and he managed the journey without stumbling so much as once.

Eleanor, when she wasn't overwhelmed by the mind-numbing coldness of her limbs, or the chattering of her teeth, or the far-away ringing in her ears, felt a little like Fay Wray struggling in the greedy palm of King Kong. She even kicked her legs helplessly in true Hollywood fashion at one point, until the man barked, 'Stop that stupid posturing. You've caused enough trouble for one day.'

Eleanor felt her eyes fill with tears. Honestly, this was too much. She had only had the child's interests at heart when she swam out after the airbed. She was a strong swimmer, and it wasn't her fault that the undertow had proved too fierce for her. She had been carried away from the child, rather than towards him. But she had been about to turn back and swim to shore to raise the coastguards when the man arrived in the boat. With a shudder she remembered the cold waters of the Irish Sea slapping against her face.

Incongruously she found herself recalling a rather boisterous party she had attended as a child, in which the climax had consisted of a custard-pie-throwing contest. Being a good shot, she had enjoyed it until a pie had landed squarely in her own face. The sensation of suffocating coldness had frightened her into a panic then. But her mother, as always, had been there to soothe her and make things better. Now all she had for comfort was this unpleasant and irascible man, who, far from soothing her, had well and truly rubbed her up the wrong way.

They had reached the top of the steep path and were crossing the cliff-top when Eleanor remembered that her things were still down on the beach.

'My bag... My clothes...' she said, protestingly. 'I can't just leave them...'

'I wouldn't worry about them,' jeered the man. 'After all, you're a heroine! No one would dare steal them. The only thing you have to worry about is the possibility of people taking small, insignificant items to keep as relics on the off-chance that you'll be beatified.'

'Stop it!' she hissed through clenched teeth. 'I haven't claimed to be anything of the sort. I can't help it if the people down there——'

'Oh, yes, you could have helped it,' he said tersely. 'You could have thanked me for saving your life, and apologised for the unnecessary trouble you caused by disobeying even the most elementary rules of safety. Maybe then some of those innocent bystanders might have learned that ploughing into dangerous waters is not necessarily the best way to go about rescuing someone.'

'But I only——'

'Yes, yes. I know. You only thought you'd swim out and tow the dear little chap to safety. If it had been the fat lady who'd swum out, or the man with the peeling nose, I would have slapped them on the shoulder, sung a round of "For he's a jolly good fellow" and nominated them for a Humane Society award.'

'But I'm different, am I?'

'Yes.'

'And how can you possibly know that?' she challenged him scathingly.

'Ah!' he gloated. 'So you admit it!'

If she hadn't been so blue with cold she would have blushed. As it was, her blood vessels were more concerned with maintaining her body temperature than with turning her face a tell-tale scarlet. He was right, of course. She really ought to have known better. But he was a stranger. Not that she hadn't noticed him about the village these past few days. It would be hard not to notice someone as good-looking as him.

She surreptitiously glanced upwards. His eyes, close to, were a strange mix of russet-brown flecked with green. Hazel, she supposed they'd be called, but the word didn't do them justice. The colour burned, clear and sharp beneath his expressive black eyebrows. She could tell that his brows were expressive, because right now they were telling her every bit as clearly as his mouth had done that he thought she was beneath contempt.

His hair too, on close inspection, turned out to be a deceptive mixture of colours. Auburn and amber and sunbleached gold mixed in the eye to make it seem an even brown at a distance. At the moment it was rumpled and damp from the sea. A heavy day's growth of stubble shadowed the strong, angular jaw—another feature which had been blurred by distance as she had watched him galloping that impressive black gelding of his along the beach at low tide, or sailing or windsurfing out in the bay.

All she knew of him was what she had glimpsed. He wouldn't even have that advantage as far as she was concerned. There was no way that a man like him would have registered her presence in the village. Which meant, fortunately, that he knew absolutely nothing about her. He couldn't know for instance, that when she had been between the ages of seven and fourteen her parents had religiously taken her to the local swimming baths every Saturday morning, and sat patiently waiting while she struggled to acquire all the certificates on offer, from the five-yard breaststroke—with one foot on the bottom, she remembered guiltily—right the way through to the higher life-saving awards.

Of course the man was right in saying that she shouldn't have attempted to swim out to the boy. She should have raised the alarm, got someone to contact the coastguard, and dragged the little dinghy—which was left on the beach for just that purpose—into the water. She knew that *now*. And she'd known it just moments before she spotted the little orange airbed with its precious cargo bobbing further and further away from the shore. But the moment she had realised what was happening, she had forgotten all her training, and had acted completely on impulse. Her powers of reasoning had only returned when it began to dawn on her that the airbed was receding instead of getting nearer. By then, of course, it had been too late to do anything except remind herself that she was a good swimmer and start to plod back to shore.

She decided it would be wiser to drop the subject of her potential eligibility for a bravery award. She was only too ready to admit she'd been in the wrong, anyway. Or, at least, she would have been, had *he* not been in such a foul mood. The way she was feeling she couldn't take any more of the caustic remarks such an admission would generate.

'Where are you taking me?' she asked, changing tack.

'Somewhere where we can get you warm and stop you shaking. If you don't come out of shock soon, I may take you to hospital.'

'That's absurd. I've told you I don't know how many times that I'm fine. I don't need to go to hospital. I'm just a bit cold, and it's hardly any wonder considering I've been in the sea.'

'So have I,' muttered the man, wryly, 'and I'm not white and shivering and threatening to pass out all the time. The temperature must be well into the eighties, if not higher. There's no trace of a breeze, and you're wrapped in a blanket. And yet you're positively blue with cold. To me that looks like shock.'

'Well, even if I am a bit shocked, then it's scarcely surprising! I did nearly...well, let's just say I did have a bit of a fright. That little boy looked so vulnerable...'

'Cut it out, eh? The fright was nothing to do with the little boy. It was all to do with going under for the second time, and remembering what you'd been told about what happens when you go down for the third time. I don't know why you're bothering to argue with me. I've told you already that you should be thanking me, but that's clearly not your style.'

'I didn't go under!' protested Eleanor fiercely, then stopped herself, reluctant to discuss the matter any more. He *was* right, though, about her not having thanked him—though he needn't have hauled her into the boat. She could have made it back to shore quite easily. Still, she ought to say something, even so. She took a deep breath.

'Oh, all right,' she mumbled. 'Thanks.' She really ought to have said it sooner, she supposed. It was just that she had, at first, saved her breath for breathing, drawing in huge, shuddering lungfuls of air as soon as she was hauled into the safety of the little boat. And then she had coughed and spluttered a bit, if she remembered aright. To be honest, her memory of the trip back to shore was a bit blurred. And all she recalled after that was being dumped unceremoniously on the sand for a few minutes, while the man restored the child to his parents. That was when the shivering started. And then the man had been there again, haranguing her about her condition, and for some reason she had found herself firmly on the defensive.

'Go on . . . I'm waiting,' said the man, a low note of sarcasm corroding his voice.

'What do you mean?'

'Well, I've never heard such a grudging thank-you in my life. I thought you might be searching your mind for a more appropriate form of expression . . .'

Eleanor took a deep breath. She was beginning to feel extremely light-headed, though the bouts of teeth-chattering seemed to have come to an end. But she was certainly a bit queasy, and had a horrible feeling that if she went on letting this man aggravate her she'd end up by throwing up over the bare, suntanned chest, peppered with dark, curling hairs, to which she was clamped by his vice-like arms. It would serve him right, of course. But on the other hand she didn't feel like facing up to any more humiliation that day. She would clearly have to acquiesce.

'Thank you, kind sir, for having been prepared to save my life had it needed saving,' she said sarcastically, and promptly passed out.

The pillow was so soft that it could only be pure duck down. It felt more like a cloud beneath her head than a pillow. And it smelled of fresh air and laundry-starch.

Eleanor curled luxuriously in the warmth of the bed for a moment, before opening her eyes abruptly. A little walnut chest of drawers to the side of the huge brass bedstead supported a softly glowing bedside lamp and a radio-alarm which informed her that it was eleven twenty-seven.

She blinked hard, trying to sort the jumble of memories that came surging back. There was a hair-drier— she remembered that quite clearly, as the buzz of the motor and the warm flow of air had kept intruding into her consciousness. And the sting of antiseptic came into the picture somewhere too. But other than that she could remember remarkably little.

Eleven twenty-nine. Oh, help! She had missed the six o'clock collection, and would only just have time to make it down to the water's edge for the one at midnight. She pushed back the bedclothes, appalled to discover that the action had exposed her breasts—her *naked* breasts. She swallowed hard, and braced herself to peep further under the clothes. As she had suspected the bottom half of her bikini was missing. She closed her eyes to meet the fog of cringing embarrassment which was enveloping her brain. Oh, no. Oh, dear. Her memory was beginning to come back.

Oh, dear. Oh, dear. Cramp. She'd had cramp and he'd massaged her calves and her thighs, chafing life back into her cold limbs. Oh, dear. It couldn't have been worse. A vision of those strong brown hands encircling her calf, stroking firmly upwards over her suntanned knee, stroking away the tension in the locked muscles, soothing away the pain, projected itself in glorious Technicolor on to her closed eyelids.

And then ... Oh, dear, perhaps it could be worse after all ... ? Then there had been the sand in the top half of

her bikini. Sand stuck clammily to the pale flesh of her
breasts. He'd sponged it away with warm water. The
vision of his hands mutated, so that now she was
watching them, still large and strong and brown,
sweeping circles around her breasts with the soft white
cloth. Round and round. Cold and damp, her nipples
had stood out, dark against the surrounding creamy skin.
Just as they were doing now at the memory. She shuddered a little, then squirmed. She remembered doing both
of those things at the time, too... Oh, dear, oh, dear.
How *could* she have been so unguarded? Finally she
opened her eyes very wide.

There was no point in thinking about all that now.
Good gracious, no! After all, it had been a sort of
medical emergency. She'd had no choice, and neither,
poor man, had he. It wasn't the sort of thing any man
would do voluntarily. Though now she came to think of
it her memory seemed to have resurrected an image of
those eyes of his gleaming sardonically, as if he relished
having her at his mercy like that. But perhaps that was
earlier on, when he'd dumped her on the beach?

Edward wouldn't have relished the job, that was for
sure, and they were, at least, engaged. She frowned at
the oddness of trying to imagine Edward undressing her.
The picture wouldn't quite gel. Of course, once they were
married he'd undress her, she supposed. Or at least, the
men in the books she read always undressed the women
with whom they were having passionate encounters. She
didn't see why Edward should be any different. No. It
was the idea of him undressing her when she was unconscious, half drowned, exhausted and in shock that
was so unconvincing. And yet Edward was so exceptionally good at looking after her. That had always been
part of his appeal...

Damn it. She would *have* to go and find that man, if she wasn't to be late, to ask to borrow a torch. The way she was feeling now, she wouldn't mind if she never clapped eyes on him ever again. She grabbed an assortment of clothes from the drawers and wardrobe. She didn't know this man from Adam. He'd brought her here against her will, had shown himself to be a bad-tempered bully, and now he'd left her naked and unconscious in his bed. He might even have drugged her for all she knew!

She let out a snort of laughter as she recognised the absurdity of her train of thought. But, even so, it would be as well to be stoutly dressed when she faced him.

By the time she had tugged on a pair of red Y-fronts, a white T-shirt and a pair of jeans several sizes too big, and far too long in the leg, she was giggling quietly to herself. A checked shirt, a thick sweater, and a pair of woolly socks completed her armour. The handsome walnut wardrobe was inset with a full-length mirror. Rolling back her sleeves, she surveyed the result. Her slender figure, long-legged, with full, rounded breasts, was completely obliterated by the layers of bulky clothes. She had nothing with which to tame her sleek, dark hair, but she twisted it into a rope at the nape of her neck, and tucked it under her jumper. At least if he did turn out to be some kind of a mad axeman he'd have a job finding her innocent young body under all that!

It was only a shame that the suntan couldn't be washed off her face. It highlighted her grey eyes, and did something for her usually pale heart-shaped face that no amount of make-up could manage. Still. At least she'd tried. She grinned at herself before setting off to find him.

'Courage, Eleanor...' she muttered to herself as she padded out on to the landing. The house seemed to be entirely in darkness. Presumably he was asleep. Good. She skidded a little on rug which lay along the polished boards. Drat! That was one way of defeating burglars, she supposed, but a bit unfair on the unwary. Still, luckily she'd managed not to topple and wake him. She had no desire to have the man think her more foolish and helpless than he clearly did already!

The kitchen, when she found it, was warm and welcoming with a gleaming red Aga. There was a big, scrubbed table, with wheel-backed chairs, a counter with a sink, a lovely dresser and two Windsor chairs, one of which was occupied by a cat. She nodded approvingly as she took in her surroundings.

A quick inspection revealed no sign of a torch. Never mind. She could manage without a torch. It had been a clear day, and the moon had been bright on the previous nights. The door, however—and the front door too when she located it and tried it—proved to be locked with no sign of a key. She glanced out of the kitchen window, reassured to spy a silvery gibbous moon beyond its mirrored reflections. She tried the window. It was a casement fitting, and opened outwards with ease. She dragged a Windsor chair in front of it, climbed up and wriggled the top half of herself through. Despite the moon it was surprisingly dark outside. She always forgot, city child that she was, how dark the countryside could be without streetlamps and car headlights to mitigate the black of night. And she wasn't helping matters by blocking the light from the window either.

She wriggled a little further forward, taking her feet off the security of the chair. Suddenly, to her horror, a dark shape, darker even than the darkness, loomed towards her out of the night and began to bark.

The dog was growling fiercely up at her appalled face. Her fingers gripped the sill in terror. Her legs flailed behind her in a wild attempt to find the chair. Then her blood curdled in her veins as she heard a key turn in a lock. Someone was breaking in to the kitchen. She couldn't go forwards and she couldn't go back. What was she to do? And then—oh, horror!—something hard and fierce bit into her waist and started dragging her back into the room.

It was almost a relief to confront the man again. For a brief moment, lodged in the window-frame, she had had visions of some yawning, nameless creature from the deep. He looked surprisingly normal when she had found her feet and turned to face him. At least he *would* have looked normal if he hadn't been laughing so hard.

'I think I will call the doctor, after all!' he gasped at last, when his shoulders had stopped quaking with mirth. 'This afternoon's experiences have obviously deranged you!'

'Stop laughing at me!' she snapped, her fist clenching into hard knots. She was having to work hard at resisting the urge to hammer at that stupidly broad chest of his with them.

'I have stopped laughing,' he said reasonably. The hazel eyes which surveyed her with such flagrant amusement glittered with green lights beneath the arched brows. The rumpled brown hair, extraordinarily thick, had been pushed back from his high forehead, revealing the hard planes of strong bone beneath the bronzed skin. He let his eyes leave her face and sweep down to her feet, clad only in his woolly socks. Then his mouth puckered, his nostrils dilated, his jutting chin jutted even further, and a resonant chuckle began to erupt from somewhere beneath his diaphragm.

'I'm sorry,' he said. 'That last statement was obviously somewhat premature.'

She stood back from him, seating herself purposefully in the chair beneath the still open window. She folded her arms and pressed her mouth into a hard line. She wasn't quite sure what the gestures were supposed to convey, but they would have to serve as she could think of absolutely nothing to say to him. She glared hard into his eyes.

'Well?' he said expectantly, when his humour had finally subsided.

'Well, what?'

'Well, aren't you going to thank me?'

'I did that earlier, if you remember. Don't get greedy.'

'No. Not for saving your life. Though a slightly more effusive show of gratitude than the one you managed wouldn't come amiss.'

'So what am I supposed to be thanking you for now?' she asked brusquely. Then she remembered how he had warmed her and dried her, not to mention *undressed* her. Of course she should be thanking him for all that. But now she had foolishly gone and given him the opportunity to spell it all out to her, which, no doubt, he would do with the greatest of delight.

'For fetching your pails of water, dear Jill,' he informed her, his face breaking into a broad and unbearably superior smile.

'It's Eleanor, actually. And you'll have to forgive me, but I don't know what you're talking about.'

'Oh, I know you don't fetch it in pail-loads. You have some weird glass apparatus for extracting it. But it's seawater, when all's said and done, isn't it? I don't suppose it will matter much that it's spent a couple of hours in a bucket, will it?'

'Er—no. I shouldn't think so. But I still don't understand . . .'

'Well, it was obvious that you were in no condition to go creeping out on to those rocks with your stopwatch and your little jars and tubes and bits of string. So I thought I'd go and get the water for you. I went at six, and then again just now at midnight. That's right, isn't it?'

'Yes. But how did you know?'

'I've been watching you.'

'Well, of all the sneaky, underhand——'

'Oh, come on. I'm not a Peeping Tom. I simply spotted you when I was walking the dog, a few mornings ago. There are only fifty-odd people living in this village. I happen to know them all. A beautiful young woman picking her way across the rocks at six in the morning came as a rather delightful surprise. What was I supposed to do? Throw myself on the grass and cover my eyes until you had gone?' He shrugged carelessly.

She glowered at him. 'Spare me the flattery,' she muttered coldly.

He crooked one eyebrow. 'Though perhaps that's exactly what I should have done?' He paused, all the warm embers of the laughter dying from his eyes. 'I see you've covered the snakes.'

She looked at him even more coldly. What on earth was he on about now? 'I beg your pardon?' she muttered haughtily.

He nodded towards her hair. 'Medusa,' he said. 'You're managing a passable imitation of her right now. Wasn't she the one with snakes for hair, the mere sight of whom could turn a man to stone?'

'Don't be so stupid,' she growled, but none the less she lifted a hand covertly to her nape and fished the swath of glossy dark brown hair out from under her jumper. His jumper. It gave off a warm, earthy smell. His smell.

'If you don't like the way I'm looking at you, perhaps you should have spared yourself the effort of dragging me out of the sea,' she countered sourly.

He turned his back to her and filled the kettle. 'Perhaps I should have done, at that,' he said curtly. Then he turned towards her and gave her a cynical smile. 'But we don't like funerals around here.'

She didn't reply. Oh, he was hateful! She had been all right. She hadn't needed his help . . . either to get back to land, or with the collections. Eleanor sighed heavily. She knew she ought to be relieved that he had fetched the water. That the project wasn't going to be spoiled because of her . . . her . . . No, it hadn't been stupidity! That man's gibes really were beginning to get to her. Because of her *impulsiveness* . . . Yes, that *was* what it had been! Anyway, she could see that, although she couldn't quite manage to feel overwhelming gratitude in the face of his condescendingly superior attitude, she *was* going to have to thank him again. Worse luck.

'Well . . . I must say . . .' she exclaimed, trying to inject a note of sincerity into her voice ' . . . it was really most enterprising and thoughtful of you to get the water for me!'

'It doesn't hurt, you know.'

'What doesn't?'

'Expressing gratitude. It doesn't damage the vocal cords, or do any kind of physical harm, so far as I know.'

'But I did thank you . . .'

'No, you didn't. You told me I was enterprising and thoughtful. I have to commend you on the accuracy of your perceptions. But it didn't sound much like an expression of gratitude to me.'

'Good grief. You do like to get your pound of flesh, don't you?'

He let a slow smile curl one corner of his mouth. Then his eyes widened slightly as if to agree...

She winced. Trust a man like him to see innuendo where there was none!

'So...?' The word trickled across the space between them.

'Oh, all right, then. Have it your own way.' She hunched her shoulders furiously before snapping, 'Thank you for getting my water. Sir!'

'Oh, you don't need to go over the top, Eleanor. I'm not a knight of the realm. Or not yet, anyway.'

'I didn't suppose for one moment that you were. It's just that I don't know your name...'

'Gilchrist Rhys,' he said, taking his hand out of his jeans pocket and thrusting it at her. 'But you can call me Gil.'

She blinked weakly at his hand, then offered hers in exchange. It was rather odd, shaking hands at this time of night, in this kitchen with two buckets of sea-water beside them on the table.

His grip was firm and dry, his hand every bit as big as she had remembered it, gripping her calf...massaging gently. He didn't free her hand after the customary few seconds, but brought it up to his lips and planted a kiss on her knuckles.

She stared at him, horrified. 'That was a very presumptuous thing to do,' she accused.

'Mmm,' he agreed, dropping her hand like a cold potato. Then he added coldly, 'It was, wasn't it? Don't do it again, Eleanor, or I won't be responsible for my actions.'

'But I didn't do anything!' she exclaimed, appalled. 'You were the one who kissed my hand.'

'Was I? Oh, yes. But only because you slipped your delicate little fingers into mine so beckoningly...so enticingly...'

'I didn't!' she cried, enraged. 'I just shook hands with you out of courtesy!'

And then she noticed the wicked sparkle in his eyes, and realised, to her horror, that she was being taken for a ride. 'Don't tell lies,' she muttered angrily.

'Lies? Now come on! I've been extremely open and straightforward with you. Whereas you, on the other hand, have been anything but——'

'What on earth do you mean? I haven't told you any-thing at all about myself! So how could I possibly have tried to mislead you?'

He arched his brows coldly. 'You were wearing that white bikini today,' he said evenly, gesturing upwards to a laundry frame, high above the Aga.

She felt herself colour beneath her tan at the oblique reference to his undressing her. 'Yes...?'

'But for the past couple of days you've been wearing a navy blue one-piece swimsuit...?'

'Er—yes...?'

'With several badges sewn on to it. Including one which represents the silver award of the National Lifesaving Association...'

'Oh.' Eleanor's eyes dropped. So he really had known that she ought to have know better... Then something occurred to her and her eyes flashed fiercely. 'So! You're an open book, are you, Mr Gilchrist Rhys? You've only spotted me in the distance in a casual sort of way, have you? Then how come you know what sort of badges I have on my swimsuit?'

He was smiling wryly at her, not the least embarrassed at having been caught out. 'You fell asleep on the beach yesterday afternoon. I just happened to walk by—close enough to recognise the badge. I did those life-saving awards when I was a kid, too. The only difference between my badge and yours is that in my case the training obviously stuck, whereas in yours... Well, it's just so much embroidery, isn't it?'

Eleanor groaned. 'OK,' she sighed. 'You win. I certainly should have known better. But no great harm was done because of my impulsiveness, so can't you just let the matter drop?'

'Stupidity, not impulsiveness.'

He might have been echoing her own thoughts. Or, more likely, Svengali-like, imposing his own thoughts on her.

'Look. I'm a strong swimmer. I thought——'

'You thought nothing!' he exclaimed sharply. 'That's the problem! That's why you nearly drowned.'

'I didn't nearly drown. Certainly the current was dragging me further away from the boy, but I could have returned to shore...'

'No, you couldn't. The tide was going out. You weren't just being pulled across the bay, but further out to sea as well. You'd soon have been swept right out of the cove. If you'd have made it to land, you'd have ended up being smashed against a sheer cliff-face.'

Eleanor stared hard at him, her face white and set. He wasn't right—he couldn't be. She was a strong swimmer. He was staring back at her, his face equally resolute, obviously waiting for a response. He clearly believed his version of events as forcefully as she did hers.

'I'll unpick my badge and send it back if it will make you happy!' she said bitterly at last.

'You're missing the point. I feel sorry for you—bloody sorry for you—for having come so close to drowning. But don't kid yourself that you're some kind of a heroine. I had to haul you out of the water before I went for the boy. What if he'd been washed into the sea during those minutes?'

He was almost shouting at her and his eyes had darkened thunderously. For a moment she looked challengingly back at him, then her gaze faltered. An image of the boy tipping off the precarious airbed into the smacking, sucking, glassy sea came into her mind. She blinked it away, forcing herself to remember the reality of the child running happily back up the beach with his parents. Of course she would have made it back to shore without his help. He was exaggerating terribly. She was not about to concede that he'd saved her life. None the less he had clearly saved her from a very unpleasant and demanding swim.

She looked away from him before saying, reluctantly, 'Have it your own way. Thank you. I suppose I was in need of some help.'

He nodded curtly, then smiled wryly and said, 'And now you can thank me for warming you through and dressing your abrasions and——'

'Yes, yes. Enough is enough. I can't help feeling that I've delivered my pound of flesh in full. I think it would be as well to draw a veil over the rest.'

He said nothing more. But he smiled. That dry, omniscient smile of his which sent fury charging back into
her veins.

CHAPTER TWO

ELEANOR watched Gil warily while she sipped at her tea. Any minute now, she was sure, he was going to start tearing a strip off her again. How on earth had she ended up drinking tea with someone who made it so plain that he not only disliked her, but positively despised her as well? She held the mug close to her chin, letting the steam rise up and soothe the frown from her face.

Eleanor wasn't used to being disliked. A cherished child, she had always gone out into the world with the confidence of one who knew she was loved, and people had responded accordingly. On the whole, she liked people and they seemed to like her in return. So what made Gil so different? The fact that she had acted foolishly from the best of motives? Surely no one could be that unforgiving... And yet *he* was.

Her tea finished, she approached the gleaming steel buckets of water on the kitchen table and proceeded to make up her filtered and unfiltered samples ready to send off to the lab the following day. She supposed she ought to thank him for bringing her box of apparatus from her tent, too, but her mouth wouldn't seem to form the words. She surveyed the six o'clock bucket for a few moments, wondering whether or not she should write a covering note to explain that it had been stagnating for some hours before being filtered.

Once she had finished she picked up the buckets and looked for a suitable place to dump the remains of the water. Gil took them from her and poured the water down the sink, then set about rinsing them thoroughly.

'You're very particular about your buckets,' she commented, watching him take a bottle of what she presumed to be disinfectant from a cupboard, and wipe the insides clean. 'Most people save that kind of attention for the family heirlooms!'

'Most people don't milk their goats into their family heirlooms,' he said drily.

'How big is your farm?' returned Eleanor, glad of the opportunity to get the conversation on to a more even footing.

'About twenty acres. It's not really a farm at all. I simply keep the goats to prevent a couple of small fields from getting overgrown. Most of the land is wooded. Then there's the river, and the paddocks for the horses. Not much, really.'

'So you're a smallholder?'

He gave a brief, caustic laugh. 'No. I employ someone to manage the land for me. I'm in marine engineering.'

'Oh. So you don't milk your own goats?'

'Not usually. But as it happens my manager is off on holiday, so I've been doing it for the past few days.'

'But normally you mend boats for a living?'

He gave a very brief, very amused laugh then. 'Not exactly. There have been Gilchrist Rhys establishments in all of the Bristol Channel ports for nearly a century now. And more recently in most of the major ports in Britain. We also fly teams of engineers to docks across the globe, patching up the odd leaking dinghy or two.'

'Leaking dinghy?' she echoed suspiciously.

'Well, merchant ships and passenger liners. Oil tankers. That sort of thing.'

'Oh...' Her voice faltered. She really had made a bit of a gaffe. But then, he had always been dressed so casually when she'd seen him. Jeans and sweatshirts and bathing trunks. Black bathing trunks, with a green flash on one side, cut below his navel and revealing a streak of dark hair, converging on the mid-line, disappearing beneath the clinging waist-band and...

'It sounds very high-powered,' she continued briskly. 'Gilchrist Rhys—Boat Menders... Hmm, I like it. I shall have to contact my PR consultants and see what they think...'

'Oh, shut up.' He was a great one for rubbing salt into open wounds. He probably hadn't used antiseptic at all on that graze on her thigh. No wonder it had stung.

'All right.'

He did. But it wasn't a comfortable silence. 'So you're quite rich, then?' she asked brightly unable to bear it.

'Yes.'

There was something about the definitive way he said it which made her suspect she'd pitched the level a little low.

'Is this your weekend cottage?'

'No. I have a chalet in the Alps for relaxation. And a little place in the West Indies.'

'Oh.' She *had* pitched it rather low, obviously. Was it five or six bedrooms she'd located upstairs? Hard to tell with all the lights off. It seemed to be a lovely house. A big old farmhouse, with lots of polished wood and quarry tiles. But not exactly the sort of home she would have picked out for a captain of industry. 'This house is superb but it's not... well, what I mean is...'

'This is how I like to live. I work hard, I play hard and I enjoy life. I also have to travel a lot. This is an easy place to manage—particularly as there are plenty of villagers who need a little part-time work. As it happens there *is* a much grander place in the family, with an extensive estate attached to it. But my parents live there. I could have them shunted off to retirement homes, I suppose, for the sake of my image. But I suspect they'd miss the entertaining and the salmon fishing and the golf.'

'Oh.' It seemed odd to think of Gil having parents, just like...well, just like Edward, for instance. Although the mention of them did make him seem a little more human. He looked to be about mid-thirties—quite young enough to have parents still enjoying life, so she didn't know why she should find the idea so odd. Perhaps it was the thought of his parents *enjoying* life that was difficult to encompass? Edward's parents were always too busy to enjoy life. Certainly they didn't see friends much or go fishing or anything. There were always roses to be pruned back to hard stumps, or net curtains waiting to be pegged on the line when the rain stopped, or plastic dashboards needing to be wiped over with a damp cloth.

Gil set the buckets to one side, then gave her a keen look. 'I rinsed them out in fresh water before collecting the sea-water, but I can't guarantee that they were wholly free of traces of sterilising solution. You'd better mention that in your letter.'

Eleanor looked at him in blank astonishment. 'What do you mean? What letter?'

'The one you'll be sending off with those samples to explain that they haven't been collected in the usual way.'

Annoyance flickered inside her. She disliked the way he seemed to be taking over her life. Although she had only minutes earlier decided to write she found herself saying, 'Oh. I—er—well, I'm not sure that I'll bother with a letter. I doubt it will make any difference. Anyway, what do you know about it all?'

'Oh, enough. It goes off to some science lab to be analysed, doesn't it? I don't have a clue as to whether the improper collection of the water or the traces of sterlising solution will make any difference to the analysis, but neither, I suspect, do you. I should think that you most certainly ought to write a covering letter so that the scientists who are in a position to judge these things can come to their own conclusions.'

He was looking at her in that disarmingly cool way again. She must have been an idiot to have warmed to him—however slightly. The idea of someone making her decisions for her when she was supposed to be on *holiday*—even if it was a working holiday—made her eyes prickle with tears of dismay. She blinked them furiously away, then shrugged with an impatient insolence, and muttered, 'Have it your own way. I'll write a note when I send them in the morning. How did you come to be so well informed, anyway?'

He smiled at her then. A smile of sharp, taunting amusement. She could see the jasper lights flickering in those keen eyes of his.

'Perhaps,' he began drily, 'as a stranger to these parts you can be forgiven for not knowing that the fastest way to broadcast your business down here is to tell Gwen Jenkins at the post office. The whole village now knows why you're sending off a small parcel marked "fragile" at the same time every day.' His face broke into a wide, cynical smile and he added, 'Actually, you should be delighted that she's spread the word.'

'Why? I mean, I don't mind everybody knowing. It's no secret. But why should I be *glad*?'

'Because rumour had it that you were a distraught wife, anxious to have a baby, and sending off samples for a pregnancy test!'

Eleanor felt her cheeks colour hotly, and she stammered, 'No! Well, really...'

'Oh, it's OK,' he continued, his face assuming an expression of wide-eyed innocence, 'I soon put them straight. I told them that you were only wearing an engagement ring, so that the gossip couldn't be right...'

'But then they would have thought that I was sending off samples because I was anxious *not* to be pregnant!' she wailed indignantly, glancing at the small diamond which glittered on her left hand, and wondering how much else he had discovered about her in three days.

'Really?' he murmured, his tongue firmly in his cheek. 'Now why on earth would they have thought something like that? People around here are very innocent, you know—not like you fast and loose Londoners.'

'We're not all——' she began to argue, then bit the words back. He was teasing her and she was falling straight into his trap. She had learned at school that being an only child made her susceptible to teasing... She never recognised the signs until too late, unlike her classmates from larger families who were masters of the art.

'Go on. Do continue. This is most interesting. We're not all what in London?' drawled Gil, his dark brows curving sardonically above his glittering eyes.

'Nothing,' she muttered, sighing pointedly.

He tipped the cat off one of the Windsor chairs and lowered his big frame into it, tilting his head back and stretching out his long legs.

'Now this is very interesting,' he murmured softly to himself, his eyes half concealed by his lowered lids. 'Why should she be sending off sea-water to be pregnancy tested? Could she be a journalist, exposing fraudulent laboratories?'

'No, I am not! And anyway, it would be pointless doing a pregnancy test on sea-water!' she exclaimed heatedly, just a split second before she realised that he was getting a rise out of her again.

'Intriguing...' he muttered. 'So why should anyone post off little bottles of sea-water to be analysed? Perhaps she has a sea-water aquarium and is so finicky about her fish that she has the water tested before refilling it? Or maybe she has friends who work in labs, and this is her version of the picture postcard. "Weather lovely. Water like this. Wish you were here." Or then again——'

'Or then again,' she interrupted crossly, 'it might just be a piece of research to support a job application!'

He seemed to lengthen fractionally in the chair. But instead of picking up on her comment he put up a hand to silence her. 'Don't say a word. The mists are beginning to clear.' His lids lowered further. 'I see a student with his leg in plaster. He has to complete some research in order to get his degree. But he can't collect his samples because of his accident. So his professor—who used to be your professor when you were a student—asks you to help...'

His eyes sprang open, very wide. 'Knock once on the table if I'm right. Twice if I'm wrong.'

'How did you know?' she asked accusingly.

'You told Gwen Jenkins. Remember?'

'Oh.'

'But what I don't understand, Eleanor, is where the job application comes in.'

'There isn't one. I haven't applied for any jobs.'

'But, Eleanor, I distinctly remember you saying——'

'Ha! Wrong! I merely suggested it as a possibility.'

'Hmm...'

'Look,' she added icily, heartily sick of being the butt of his warped sense of humour, 'it's been very nice talking to you but I'd better get back to my tent. I've got to be up at the crack of dawn.'

Gil shook his head, and pressed his lips into a thin line. 'You're staying here tonight. Shock's a funny thing—I'm not having you go back to that tent alone tonight.'

'Since when have you dictated my life?'

'Oh, since about three o'clock this afternoon, I'd say. Wouldn't you?'

'Well, in that case the sooner you stop the better. I'm quite capable of managing alone. Thank you very much for all you've done, but——'

'But nothing. The radio alarm next to the bed you were in is set for five-thirty. You can wake me when you get up. I'll be in the room opposite. That should be early enough for you, huh? And, in case you were thinking of arguing, the house is locked for the night, and I always sleep with the key under my pillow. Or, at least, starting tonight I shall be.'

'There's always the window,' said Eleanor defiantly, then immediately wished she hadn't. The ignominy of being dragged back through it was still too fresh to countenance.

Gil threw back his head and let out a guffaw of laughter. 'Jip is an exceptionally good guard dog,' he said, 'as you've already discovered! You can try it if you like, but I don't fancy your chances. His kennel is just below that window.'

Eleanor stood up, and took a few paces away from the offending window as the memory of the fearsome sight of the black dog looming up out of the darkness trickled back into her mind.

The jeans, several sizes too large, had eased down a bit while she had been sitting, and now slid with unholy haste down to mid-thigh level in true slapstick fashion. She made a grab for them, and speedily yanked them up, but not before Gil's face had crumpled once again into uncontained mirth at the brief appearance of his red Y-fronts, amid the muddle of shirt-tail and T-shirt.

'You see,' he spluttered, 'you *must* still be in shock. Nothing else could account for your choosing such an unusual assortment of clothes on a lovely warm evening like this. Now go to bed before I ring for the men in white coats to come and take you away!'

She was trapped. Every time she tried to assert herself in front of him she ended up looking an even bigger fool. Honestly, he was quite horrible! Thank goodness there were men like Edward in the world. He would never dream of laughing at her. At least, not in that tormentingly arrogant way.

She glanced across at him as she gathered together the bundle of clothes he had brought from her tent. He had his back to her and was rinsing out their tea mugs at the sink. His shoulders were broad beneath the flecked wool of his fisherman's jersey, and, as he bent his head to the task, she saw that the nape of his neck was burned dark by the sun. A small, endearing duck's tail of brown, wavy hair curled below his hairline, clinging to the smooth, tanned skin. She hastily swung around and made for the door to the hallway. She didn't want him to find her staring at him like that. Goodness only knew what kind of supercilious comment it would draw from those twisted lips of his. He seemed determined to treat her like an idiot, and she had no desire to give him any more fodder for his sharp tongue.

*   *   *

She slept heavily and dreamlessly, finding it almost impossible to haul herself awake when the radio-alarm pierced her consciousness with a discussion on agricultural accountancy. In the end she managed to put her feet to the floor—though it was a further minute or so before she could unglue her eyelids. She dressed like an automaton, and padded downstairs to make some coffee. Coherent thought was out of the question.

Gil was already in the kitchen, looking alert and cheerful. He smiled a greeting as she slumped into a chair, propping up her head on her hands, while her elbows skidded outwards across the table-top.

'You look as if you slept well!' he remarked, reaching into a cupboard for a couple of mugs.

She let her eyes travel over his muscular frame. He had his back to her, and she found her gaze resting on the bold curve of his buttocks beneath the worn denim of his jeans. Embarrassed to catch herself viewing him so...well, so lingeringly, she hastily looked away.

'I slept rather heavily,' she admitted at last, her words sounding oddly muffled as she moved her reluctant lips.

'Hmm...' he murmured, knowingly. 'Shock takes it out of you a bit. It can leave you feeling quite woolly for a few days.'

'I don't feel at all woolly,' she lied. 'I just slept a bit heavily, that's all.'

He crossed over to her, then placed his hands flat on the table in front of her and, supporting his weight on his arms, he bent down until his eyes were level with hers. He stared deeply into her eyes. She stared back, feeling slightly nervous. Why was he looking at her like that? She could hear him breathing—even feel the warmth of his soft breath on her face. Surely he wasn't going to *kiss* her? Her heart started to pound erratically, and she hastily shifted her gaze from his eyes to the middle distance, which turned out to be obscured by the taut muscles of his arms, emerging from the short sleeves of his navy polo shirt.

'Look back into my eyes...' he ordered.

She blew out a long breath, quaking inwardly with relief. That was *not* the voice of a man about to take unmentionable liberties. Thank goodness. She looked back uncertainly.

He continued to stare deeply for a few moments, then said, 'It's OK. Your pupils are the same size.'

'Is there any reason why they shouldn't be?' she asked.

He had turned back to the counter to pour fresh coffee into the mugs. 'Not in the usual way of things, no. But it did occur to me that you might have hit your head when I shoved you into the boat yesterday. Unequal pupils are a sign of concussion.'

'Shoved?' she murmured a little querulously. She thought she remembered him *dragging* her into the boat...

'Yes. I had to get into the water and heave you up from behind, in the end,' he explained patiently.

'But I thought...' She shook her head, confused.

'Don't you remember?' he asked quietly, coming to sit opposite her.

She shook her head, dismayed. The memories were all a bit foggy, but she had been certain that he had merely given her a hand into the boat from inside.

'I pulled you half in,' he said neutrally. 'But you didn't have the strength to help yourself right in. So I popped over the side and gave you a leg-up.' He was smiling, and for once the smile lacked its searing edge.

'Oh...' she said bleakly, taking the mug and lifting it blindly to her lips.

*   *   *

The air on the cliff-top was raw with the freshness of early morning. The collection made, she set her box of samples on the coarse, dew-wet grass, and then impulsively sat down beside them. The cool, damp turf prickled against her skin and set her heart singing with pleasure. The muzziness had quite gone, and never, ever, she was sure, had she felt more gloriously and uproariously pleased to be alive. Impulsively she lay down and rolled over and over, so that her hair, her skin, her clothes drank in the soft morning dew. At last she lay spread-eagled on her back, watching the peachy mist over the horizon, and the silver mirror of the sea.

She propped her head up on her elbow, the better to watch the rise and fall of the waves on the firm crescent of sand. The water peaked and tumbled, spreading soapy fingers on to the golden-brown beach. She found herself catching at her breath so that she inhaled and exhaled in unison with the sea. This was what must be meant by feeling at one with nature. How was she ever going to bear returning to London?

She grimaced slightly. No point in thinking about that now. She still had eight lovely days left, and she planned to make the most of them, especially having had half of yesterday spoiled by that malicious man. She drove him from her mind, letting her eyes drift lazily out over the shimmering surface of the sea.

There was a rock out in the bay. A huge, towering rock, almost as far out as the headland. With a convulsive flash of horror Eleanor realised that she knew exactly what the far side of that rock looked like—barnacle-encrusted, blue-black with mussels, ragged with seaweed, breaking the pale line of the beach beyond. She knew what it looked like because she had been there. Yesterday. But if she'd been carried out that far, way out beyond the rock, then Gil was right. She would certainly have drowned. She scrambled to her feet, her heart hammering wildly.

Now she wasn't just happy to be alive. She was overwhelmingly grateful to be alive. So Gil really *had* saved her life after all . . . ? Why had she resisted the realisation for so long? Her head bowed. Her skin darkened with the unfamiliar, burning heat of real shame. She had been unbelievably rude to him, denying the truth of everything he said. Now, as she recalled being carried up the cliff path, she longed to bury her face against the broad, muscular chest and sob out her gratitude. She could almost smell the male tang of his skin, so powerful was the image. She could almost feel the darkly curling hairs rubbing roughly against her cheek. Her skin prickled uncomfortably at the thought, and she found herself almost choking for air.

As soon as she was confident that she had brought herself under control she set off back to his place to thank him. This time she would do it properly, with every ounce of grace she could muster. No matter that she dreaded the encounter. No matter that he would look at her in that mocking way. He could think what he liked of her. It was, anyway, no more than she deserved.

She saw him in the paddock, before she got anywhere near the house. The black gelding was nuzzling his hand, and the pretty little grey mare was nudging him playfully in the small of his back. She stood silently for a moment, watching. The morning sun was still casting long shadows across the grass.

He looked at ease with the horses. Loose-limbed, long-legged, he moved nimbly away from the mare, turning easily to fondle her mane as he did so. And it was as he turned that he spotted her. He raised a hand in salute, then came striding across the field in her direction.

Suddenly her mouth felt uncomfortably dry and her pulses quickened alarmingly. His thumbs were hooked loosely in the pockets of his jeans, his broad shoulders hunched. What would she say? How could she explain what she felt?

He smiled as he drew near, his teeth flashing white against the sun-browned planes of his face.

'Hi!' she said uneasily.

'Good,' he said confidently. 'You're back just in time for breakfast.'

She looked up at him. 'What?'

'You heard me. I'm taking you back to the house for a slap-up breakfast. New laid eggs, home-cured bacon, magnificent field mushrooms. With porridge to start and toast and honey to finish. The only thing that won't be home-grown is the coffee. That comes from Kenya.'

He caught hold of her wrist and drew her reluctantly towards him.

'But I can't possibly——' she blurted, then added in a tight little voice, 'Thank you very much, but I've already had breakfast.'

'Really? So what did you have besides the coffee I made you earlier? Or would you rather not answer that?'

'I—er—I've actually come to say——'

'Precisely. You're avoiding my question, eh? Evasions, again, Eleanor! Tut, tut. You haven't had anything, have you? No wonder you're so thin.' And he released her wrist, letting his hands reach out and slip under her loose white T-shirt to pinch teasingly at the flesh of her midriff. It was an innocent enough gesture, clearly intended only to taunt her for her slender build. It was Eleanor's body that made it into something more . . . more suggestive.

The sensation that flooded through her at the tantalising nip of his fingers on her unprepared flesh took her quite by surprise. She stopped breathing, her mouth dropped open and her grey eyes became dark and languorous as a charge of desire exploded within her. Edward had held her many times, but never had she felt anything remotely like this. It was as if a tiny flame had suddenly burst into life and was sending a molten heat roaring upwards, to cascade in burning fragments throughout her whole being. His hands slid round to the small of her back, where they remained, lightly resting beneath the soft, clinging mantle of her still damp T-shirt.

Her skin seemed to hug her more tightly, and when she followed Gil's mocking eyes downwards she saw that her nipples had tightened into firm buds, which pushed embarrassingly and urgently at the soft fabric.

'Now, who would have believed that?' murmured Gil laconically, lifting his eyes. Hers travelled up to meet them, anxious to hold his gaze away from the telling peaks of her breasts. His eyes were momentarily dark, then lightened into glittering nut-brown mirrors, at exactly the same moment as his hands slid upwards across her back, caressing her skin lightly, almost experimentally. He rested the broad palms of his hands against her shoulder-blades, and then, tantalisingly, drew the edge of one thumb down her spine to her waist.

Infuriatingly, she shivered perceptibly as a fresh wave of sensation shimmered across her skin.

'Excuse me,' she said huskily, pushing him away, 'but you really have got an enormous cheek . . .'

'Oh, come on,' he said, his eyebrows arching humorously. 'I wasn't trying to seduce you . . .'

'Yes, well...' she muttered, biting furiously at the corner of her mouth. She hadn't for one moment thought that he had meant anything by his light, frivolous pinching. It was she who had made a sexual moment of it. Why on earth had her treacherous body responded like that, without first consulting her conscious mind? Something animal and instinctive within her had obviously recognised the fact that she owed him her life. She had never before experienced such a fierce surge of desire—had not known it was possible for arousal to flame so abruptly and inappropriately.

It was nice cuddling up to Edward and kissing him. But they had decided to wait until they were married for anything more, and she had always assumed that she would be able to unleash her desires on their wedding night, when the time was right. She had not realised that they could swim free, uninvited, like this. But then Edward had never saved her life. No doubt it was the heady mixture of shock and relief and gratitude that had caused it...

'Now come along,' he urged amicably, putting one hand on her shoulder and pushing her towards the gate. 'I'm starving...'

'I told you. I've already had breakfast,' she protested, shrinking out from under his hand, which had managed to rekindle that infuriatingly persistent flame.

'Nonsense. Stop making difficulties where there are none, and get a move on.'

'What on earth makes you think you have a right to make me go anywhere with you?'

He shrugged amiably. 'I don't have a right. But you do have an obligation, as it happens. As you seem to find it so hard to express your thanks in the conventional way, I've decided that you can show me your gratitude in a more practical manner. You owe me one, Eleanor. Remember?'

'How dare you?' she cried. 'How dare you think that just because you saved my life I would...would...?' She tailed off, unable to spit out the words which hovered on her tongue.

He threw back his head and gave a short, astonished laugh. 'No. No. I didn't mean what you obviously thought I meant!' And he laughed again, then added, 'Believe it or not, I don't exactly relish the idea of carting you off to my bed and making mad, passionate love to you. You're far too much of a prude and much too bolshie to be any kind of fun. No. I simply want to butter you up to ask another kind of favour from you. Which, sooner or later, you are going to have to admit you owe me.'

Eleanor screwed up her face as she positively cringed with embarrassment. She had indeed assumed that he had meant that she owed him a sexual favour. This was awful. How could she have made a mistake like that? And, to cap it all, he hadn't even had the grace to pretend to relish her error. Not that she wanted him to want her like that... But to come right out and say that he wouldn't enjoy having her in his bed! Oh, the man was impossible!

He had succeeded in making her feel an utter fool, yet again. As the humiliation waned she realised that she hadn't even got round to thanking him properly yet. And now it would look as if she was only doing it because he had prompted her, yet again. Still, there was no avoiding it. She took a deep breath. She was going to have to say her piece, but the timing couldn't be worse. Quite frankly, all she wanted to do was slap his complacent face very, very hard.

'Actually,' she said with some difficulty, 'Well, actually, Gil, the truth has already dawned. I honestly hadn't realised until I looked at the sea this morning how far out the current had carried me. You were right. I would never have made it back to shore alone. I'm sorry I was so ungrateful. I was a complete idiot and it's only thanks to you that I'm alive this morning. So... Thank you... very much.' She looked up at him, feeling astonishingly lighter for having said the words.

He surveyed her quizzically, his head tilted to one side. 'You're welcome,' he said, sounding genuinely pleased, if a little surprised. 'But don't think that speech lets you off the hook. You're still going to have breakfast with me, after which I shall tell you exactly what you can do to repay my extraordinary bravery and kindness. Now come along, or it will be lunchtime.'

He started walking. There was nothing she could do but follow. To have refused would have made her seem unbelievably churlish.

His farmyard was a pretty, cobbled affair, surrounded by an array of whitewashed barns and outbuildings, some of them neatly thatched. Eleanor's eyes flicked across to the kitchen window. There was no sign of a kennel, either beneath it or anywhere else.

'Where's the dog?' she said cagily.

'Oh, he's probably snoozing in the sun somewhere. Old Jip's pretty ancient, you know. He doesn't get up to much these days, especially since he lost a few teeth.'

'But last night you said he was a vicious guard dog!' said Eleanor indignantly.

Gil laughed. 'Did I? Oh, dear. I can't have been concentrating. Mind you, he *is* rather good at barking.'

'Beast...' she muttered.

'Only technically,' he said, deliberately misunderstanding her. 'He's a good deal more human than most of the people I know. Anyway, I was simply protecting you from your own wilful nature with an expedient little white lie.'

'I don't need protecting,' she complained wearily. 'I'm fine in the tent. I'm within shouting distance of the Prossers' house and, anyway, I'm sure I'm more at risk living in London than I am down here. I've been sleeping alone in tents in the wilds for ten years, since I was in my mid-teens. I used to do geography and geology field-trips when I was at school, and I did the Duke of Edinburgh's award too, not to mention numerous solitary field-trips when I was at university. I've never allowed myself to get nervous. Waking up alone to the smell of earth and canvas and the sound of the dawn chorus is my idea of heaven.' She paused, then added assertively, 'It may have its dangers, but if you don't close your eyes to some of life's risks you never get to reap its rewards, do you?' She glanced up at him, waiting to answer the challenge.

But the challenge never came. Instead, the eyes that met hers from beneath the dark, furrowed brows glinted out their unmistakable approbation.

He led the way into the kitchen, gesturing her to sit at the big, scrubbed table. A jam-jar of nasturtiums stood gaily in the centre, almost as if he'd been expecting company.

'Oh, I don't doubt you're right,' he said. 'I'm not worried about you sleeping in the tent alone in the general way of things. It's just that you weren't exactly in good shape earlier in the day, and I felt you oughtn't be on your own for the first night at least.'

'Oh,' responded Eleanor, rather nonplussed. She was too much in the habit already of disputing everything he said to be able to think of a reply when he came out with something so eminently reasonable.

He went over to the dresser and opened one of the drawers. He took out a writing pad, pen, envelope and stamp, and placed them neatly before her on the table.

'Do you want to use these? You can get on with that letter while I cook breakfast,' he said.

Eleanor glowered as she picked up the pen and opened the pad. 'I used to feel like this when my dad sat me down to do my thank-you letters after Christmas,' she muttered resentfully.

'Hmm. I can see that Christmas must have been a problem for you, given that you have such an aversion to saying thank you. But this is just a common or garden letter of explanation. It shouldn't be a problem, assuming you know how to write?'

He was goading her again, but as usual her retort was out of her mouth before she realised she was being teased. 'Of course I can write! I've got a first-class honours degree in geology, as it happens!'

He gave a low whistle. 'I'm impressed. A first, no less! So you're capable of being intelligent as well as beautiful...'

'Don't try to flatter me. I'm not that much of an imbecile.'

'And don't *you* go fishing for compliments. I'm not into playing those sorts of games. You can't try telling me that you've got this far in life without realising the effect you have on men,' he said rather acidly.

'But I——' She stopped herself. Of course she wasn't beautiful, but there was something in his response to her protest that rather suggested that he meant it. She sud-

denly longed to jump up and study herself in a mirror.
Her mother had often said that she looked quite attractive when she took a bit of trouble with her appearance, and her father had occasionally commented
that she was looking particularly handsome when she
was dressed up for a party or something. And Edward,
of course, never failed to comment on her appearance,
letting her know when she had gone over the top with
a new outfit or make-up or hairstyle. They had all reassured her time and again that she was a perfectly good-
looking woman. But none of them had ever said that
she was beautiful.

She shrugged, telling herself that such things were all
in the eye of the beholder, anyway. But that line of
thought ran into a ditch when she realised that as Gil
had such a low opinion of her he was hardly likely to
behold her as beautiful. Oh, well. Yet another of life's
unfathomable mysteries. She licked the seal of the envelope and stuck it down firmly.

She was finding it hard to take her eyes off him. Any
minute now he might turn around and find her staring
at him. She ran her tongue over her lips, searching her
mind for something to say to break the spell.

'I'm sorry about yesterday,' she said at last.

'That's OK,' he replied, his attention on the cooking.

'No. Really. I can't apologise enough.'

'Don't mention it. It's over and done with.'

'Yes, but I feel awful about the way I reacted. I am
sorry.'

He paused, then turned his head, flashing her one of
his sardonic smiles. 'Well, at least your parents did half
a job when it came to teaching you your manners.'

'What do you mean?' she muttered cagily, feeling fairly certain that she was about to be treated to another dose of his acerbic wit.

'They taught you to say sorry! In fact, they must have taken so much time teaching you to say the word that they never got round to teaching you how to say thank you.'

'Surely there's nothing wrong with apologising? I might have known you'd turn it into another way of getting at me,' she said with a sigh of resignation.

'I'm not getting at you, Eleanor, believe it or not. I'm getting at them. They should have told you that you should apologise only when an apology is required, but that you can say thank you any day of the week.'

'I don't know what you think gives you the right to speak about my parents like that. You know nothing at all about them!' she said archly, firmly suppressing a broth of emotions which bubbled dangerously inside. She knew her parents had been over-protective. But they had done their best, and done it all with overwhelming love. It wasn't their fault that she wasn't the shrinking violet of a daughter that the laws of inheritance ought to have delivered to them. They would have been the world's most perfect parents if only she'd been more like them.

'Really? But I know you, Eleanor. So I have clues. You are, after all, their child. Their life's work.'

'No, I'm not! I'm my own person, thank you very much. Not some kind of Frankenstein's monster. And anyway, you hardly know me at all. So how you have the nerve to pronounce upon my character in that insufferably omniscient way defeats me!' she burst out hotly.

He gave a wry smile. 'Don't I know you? No, I suppose I don't. Though I feel as if we've been sitting in this kitchen arguing for an eternity...' He paused, and took his eyes off the frying-pan for long enough to flash her an amused look. 'But if you concede that I'm omniscient, then why are you bothering to dispute anything I say?'

He ran his fingers through his thick hair. 'Anyway, omniscient or not, I *do* know that you're the most contradictory person I've ever met!'

'And just what is that supposed to mean?'

He shrugged. 'You're very good at saying sorry, but hopeless at saying thank you. You're bold enough to go climbing out of windows at dead of night, but frightened of dogs.'

'I'm not...' she muttered, but he was too wrapped up in his thoughts to listen. Oh, well, let him go ranting on if it amused him. She wasn't going to be made a fool of again.

'You're brave enough to come to an isolated village all alone, and stay in a tent with only the earthworms for company, and go collecting water at dead of night. But you're frightened that the lady in the post office might think you're pregnant——'

'All right. All right. Point taken. That's enough,' she interrupted valiantly, concerned that he might mention the business of the rescue attempt. And yet there hadn't really been the contradiction he'd assumed. Her certificates had all been earned in the glassy waters of a swimming-pool. She'd never once until this past week gone swimming in the tidal waters of the sea. Her parents had never allowed her.

He laughed. 'Someone has made you a mass of contradictions, Eleanor, dear. So strong and forthright and fearless at times, and then so prickly and defensive at others.' He hesitated, slyly. 'Or maybe it's your boyfriend who's made you like this? Come to think of it, it makes more sense. After all, your parents created you beautiful and brave... Why should they want to spoil the effect by——?'

'Don't be stupid!' she burst out, shocked by his insincere flattery into loosing the guard on her tongue.

He crossed the kitchen, a suggestion of a smile hovering around his lips. Then he reached out and took her hand in his, lifting it to his mouth. Softly, almost delicately, he began to kiss the tips of her fingers. Her skin prickled at the breathy sensation, and her stomach fluttered expectantly, until she snatched her hand away, nursing it across her chest and glaring at him in outrage.

He gave a low laugh. 'What's the matter, Eleanor? Aren't you used to being courted? Doesn't old What's-his-name tell you that you're beautiful and kiss your fingertips?'

'It's none of your business,' she declared crossly, relieved that she had stopped herself in time from blurting out the truth. Which was, of course, that Edward would sooner grow wings and fly than behave like that. He was gentle and loving and kind, but like lots of men he didn't go in for open displays of affection. Or at least not of that kind.

Gil's head was cocked slightly to one side. 'Ah... So he doesn't, does he?' he said speculatively. 'Oh, dear. Yes, I think he must be the problem after all...'

'Oh, do be quiet,' she said through clenched teeth. 'You're crazy. You don't know anything about him at all. Not that lack of information has stopped you from assassinating my character. But I don't see why I should have to listen to a similar load of drivel about Edward.'

He had turned back to the Aga, clearly indifferent to her remarks. But at least he didn't make any more unkind comments. Inwardly Eleanor was seething. Fancy his accusing Edward of making her—what was it?—oh, yes, prickly and defensive! Honestly! It would be blindingly obvious to a ... a stuffed antelope that it was Gil himself who made her like that! And *still* she found her eyes drawn to the curve of his jaw ... the dark shadow of his chin ... She must be losing her senses!

'A geologist?' said Gil lightly, clattering around at the Aga, taking pans from cupboards and cracking huge brown speckled eggs into a teacup before plopping them into the sizzling fat. 'Now that must be a really interesting job.'

'Well, actually I'm not working as a geologist, despite my qualifications. I did an extra year at college and trained in careers guidance,' she explained, hoping against hope that he wouldn't have anything critical to say about *that*.

He turned his back on the large cast-iron frying-pan to survey her. 'Why on earth did you do that? With such a good degree surely you wouldn't have had any trouble in finding work in your specialty?'

Ah, well. She might have known there was no escaping his questions. 'Oh, careers guidance is very interesting,' she said in what she hoped was a confident and buoyant tone of voice. 'I work with school-leavers, and find it very challenging. I've been doing it for over a year now. I love it. Really. I honestly do. No regrets at all.'

Gil blew out a great sigh and turned back to the Aga.

'Just what is that sigh supposed to signify?' she snapped, unable to conceal her irritation any longer.

'Oh, Eleanor. Why are you so defensive all the time? Why can't you just come out and admit you've made a mistake? Surely it isn't too late to get a job as a geologist?'

'But you couldn't be more wrong!' she protested vehemently. 'Helping young people find their niche in life—knowing that you're setting them on the road to a happy life, which is right for them—it's . . . it's very rewarding.'

'I'm sure it must be very good for *your* soul, making certain that they don't make the same mistake as you . . .'

'But I *haven't* made a mistake,' she groaned.

He was silent.

'Being a geologist is no picnic,' she asserted uncertainly. 'Sometimes you have to work in very primitive and uncomfortable conditions.'

'Like staying out in the wilds in a tent?' he replied ironically.

'Yes! I mean . . . No. I mean . . . Sometimes you have to work on oil-rigs and so on,' she returned.

'I wouldn't have thought that would have bothered an intrepid swimmer like you. And anyway, there must be plenty of jobs which don't involve much fieldwork?'

'Why do you insist on tying me in knots? You're deliberately misinterpreting everything I say, trying to make out that I've taken some kind of wrong turning in my life. Honestly, the arrogance of it! You don't even know me. I'll have you know that I couldn't be happier. I'm absolutely one hundred per cent happy with my life! So there!'

'Oh, really?' said Gil acerbically, setting a bowl of creamy porridge in front of her. It was crusted with dark brown sugar and laced with a generous helping of thick cream. 'It's odd you should say that because you don't actually sound very happy most of the time.'

She glared at the porridge, trying to summon up the resolution to storm out. Her stomach was rumbling. What with one thing and another she hadn't really eaten since lunchtime the previous day. She picked up a spoon and took a mouthful. She could always storm out after the porridge. It tasted absolutely wonderful.

'So if you're so happy in careers guidance, why are you applying for jobs with a scientific background?'

'I told you. I haven't applied for any jobs.' She bit her lip. It was only half the truth. She'd contacted her old professor to ask if he'd give her a reference if something suitable came up. He'd hesitated, then had said that he'd be happy to, but she'd do her cause a lot of good if she had some recent fieldwork to back up an application. It was then he'd suggested helping the marine biology student. It wasn't her own field, but that didn't really matter. She'd jumped at it.

She'd been desperate for an opportunity to get away from everyone and try to assess what she was doing with her life. Twelve days at the seaside on her own sounded like just the break she needed. Perfect, in fact. Take Edward, for instance. Her parents thought the world of him, but lately she had had one or two doubts. Doubts which, if nothing else, the odious Gil Rhys was inadvertently dispelling. Comparisons themselves might be odious, but in some cases they could be very enlightening...

She spooned up her porridge. 'Mmm,' she found herself saying, her nerves soothed by the delicious concoction. 'This is fantastic! Not a bit like my mother's grey, watery stuff.'

He leaned back in his chair and smiled. The lines running from cheekbone to jaw deepened and curved, so that he seemed roguishly dimpled. 'This is my own special recipe, and a closely guarded secret. Play your cards right, kid, and you could get it for breakfast every day...'

She bent her head over the bowl, unable to think of a reply, and fearful that she might be blushing again. She wished he wouldn't tease her so. She always came off worst. Edward never did. Guiltily she recalled that she often teased him... And he loathed it. In future she'd try to stop herself. She could see that they were going to get on much better as soon as she returned to London.

Gil gave her a wry look as he cleared the bowls away and took two heaped plates from the Aga where they had been keeping warm. The bacon was crisp, the dark yolks of the eggs glistened, the mushrooms were huge and dark, and the tomatoes were lightly fried and sprinkled generously with fresh herbs. A stack of freshly made toast joined the jar of nasturtiums in the centre of the table, and with it a pat of pale, fresh butter and a jar of thick, fragrant honey. The coffee had bubbled and perked for long enough, and was brought to the table with two mugs and a jug of the same fresh cream which had graced the porridge.

Suddenly Eleanor's bad mood departed. She didn't in the least want to storm out—or, at least, not until she had feasted on this delectable spread. She reminded herself that she owed Gil a lot—that he had really been very kind and attentive. If he made her feel small all the time, then it was simply because they were such incompatible personalities. Perhaps if she tried to be a bit more gracious they could avoid knocking sparks off one another until the end of the meal at least. Then he could tell her about the favour he wanted from her, she could make up her mind whether or not to comply, and they could part on reasonable terms.

CHAPTER THREE

JIP was barking ferociously out in the yard. Although the noise was fearsome, Eleanor didn't turn a hair. She suddenly felt very relaxed and at home. She had been silly to let the dog frighten her the previous evening. She rather liked animals, though she'd had very little contact with them over the years. It was the dark, more than anything, that had made it all seem so scary.

Gil put down his knife and fork, and craned his neck to see out of the open door.

'Someone's coming...' he commented. 'Jip only barks when strangers arrive.'

He leaned back in his chair to gain a better view, tilting it on two legs, his long frame stretched out languidly.

'It's a pompous man in a suit...' he said. 'A man with yellow hair and skin like a new-born piglet. He's petrified of Jip.'

Eleanor forced her eyebrows to pucker disapprovingly, but inwardly she was suppressing a giggle. She could almost picture the man from Gil's brief description.

'He's got a grey BMW...' he added, leaning still further back to peer out of the doorway.

Eleanor's frown deepened and the bubble of relaxed good humour evaporated. 'I think it might be Edward,' she murmured, dropping her gaze to her plate and trying to concentrate on her food. Oh, help. What on earth was Edward—if it was indeed him—doing down here?

It was indeed Edward. He tapped brusquely on the open door, and stepped in without waiting to be invited.

'Hello,' smiled Gil with a surprising air of amicable good humour.

Edward didn't reply, but looked long and hard at Gil through his baby-blue eyes. It had been mean of Gil to comment so derisively on the fairness of his skin. There had been nearly two weeks of unbroken sunshine now, and Edward, who never managed to tan, had none the less well and truly caught the sun.

After waiting for a few moments for a response to his greeting, Gil raised one eyebrow quirkily, picked up his knife and fork and resumed eating.

Eleanor's mouth was fully occupied in crunching up a piece of deliciously salty and crisp bacon rind. Speech was out of the question. She tried to smile with her eyes at Edward, who was positively gawping at the rather cosy spectacle of Eleanor and Gil, bathed in a pool of mote-filled sunshine, facing each other across the breakfast table.

'Eleanor!' he exclaimed reprovingly, at last. 'All that cholesterol!'

Eleanor hastily swallowed, and looked up guiltily at him.

'It's OK,' said Gil reassuringly. 'A blow-out every now and then won't hurt. It's we men who really have to watch our diets. Particularly if we have a tendency to gain weight.'

Edward's eyes roamed over Gil's well-muscled but spare frame before dropping to his own thickening waistline. 'Now look here...' he said tartly. 'What's going on?'

'Nothing!' exclaimed Eleanor, wondering frantically how best to go about explaining things. For goodness' sake... it was all so innocent. Gil had practically had to drag her in, and all they were doing was eating breakfast. She couldn't imagine why she should be feeling so... so compromised! 'This is Gil, Edward... He invited me——'

But Gil cut across her, saying genially, 'Well, actually, we're having breakfast. Why don't you sit down and join us for a cup of coffee?'

'You must be joking!' spluttered Edward, then turned to Eleanor and said, 'Come along, Eleanor. You can explain all this later. I need to talk to you.'

Eleanor flushed. She had never known the normally mild Edward take this kind of aggressive stance before. It flashed across her mind that he must be jealous. She swallowed a smile. If only he knew how little cause he had! But she couldn't help wishing that Edward were handling things with Gil's civility. It was ironic that Gil should now be so very charming towards Edward, when he had been so persistently unpleasant towards *her* until Edward's appearance. It was as if the men had swapped personalities.

'Please, Edward,' she said evenly. 'This is all quite innocent, and I'm in the middle of my meal. Why don't you have some coffee and I'll explain?'

'You don't need to explain anything,' said Edward bitterly. 'The woman at the post office told me that you'd spent the night with *him*!' and he jerked his chin disdainfully at Gil.

'Gwen Jenkins told you *that*?' asked Gil severely. 'How odd. She's certainly always generous with her information, but rarely inaccurate. I find it hard to believe that she would have implied what I think you might be implying, which, in any case, I can assure you, is very far from the truth. Eleanor spent the night under my roof simply because she was a little under the weather.'

'Well...' said Edward, with a little less certainty. 'Maybe she didn't exactly say...' He paused for a moment as if reassessing matters, then composed his handsome features into a gentle smile which he turned directly on Eleanor.

'She also said that you saved a child from drowning yesterday, darling. Congratulations!' and he leaned forward and kissed her on the cheek, sliding into the chair beside her. He placed an arm protectively around her shoulder.

Eleanor drew away slightly. Normally she would have found Edward's sweet gestures delightful. But in front of Gil they seemed out of place. Undoubtedly it was because she was going to have to disabuse Edward of his touching faith in her bravery, and set the record straight. It wasn't that she minded that—after all, it was no more than the truth. But she wished she didn't have to do it under Gil's unfaltering and coolly appraising gaze.

She took a deep breath, and then said steadily, 'I'm afraid Mrs Jenkins was quite wrong about that, Edward. It's true that I foolishly swam out to try to rescue a small boy who was being carried out to sea on an airbed. But far from saving him I got into difficulties myself. We have Gil here to thank for the fact that both the child and I are alive and well this morning.'

Gil's expression was impassive. Edward's glance wavered between Eleanor's shamed flush and the unyielding planes of Gil's face. He smiled at Eleanor again and squeezed her shoulder.

'Well, be that as it may, I'm very proud of you, darling. You were a very brave girl!'

Eleanor dropped her eyes to her plate, and turned her knife slowly in her hand. 'I was an idiot, Edward. I should have known better. I ended up jeopardising other people's lives,' she said in a low voice.

'You're so wonderfully modest!' he responded, leaning across and planting another kiss on her cheek.

'No, she's not,' cut in Gil abrasively. 'She's simply being honest with herself for once.'

Edward looked at him with cold blue eyes. 'I beg your pardon?' he said icily.

Gil got lazily to his feet and went to fetch a mug from the dresser. He returned to the table and set it in front of Edward. He then filled it with hot, fresh coffee from the pot, pushing the jug of cream and bowl of brown sugar towards him.

'Caffeinated. Help yourself to cholesterol and carbohydrate,' he drawled, adding, with equal nonchalance, 'Why don't you take Eleanor seriously? You should. She's right, you know.'

'Now look here!' barked Edward. 'I won't have you insulting my fiancée like this!'

'He wasn't insulting me...' muttered Eleanor, but neither of the men seemed to be listening.

Gil gave a slight, insolent shrug. He smiled wryly at Eleanor then said, 'Your marriage isn't going to last long at this rate. You'll end up fighting to the death over who writes the thank-you letters for the wedding presents.'

Eleanor almost let out an unthinking laugh. Luckily she caught herself in time. She began to burn with embarrassment for Edward as it became clear he had no more intention of being grateful to Gil than she had had the previous day.

'Edward,' she whispered fiercely, twisting out from under his arm, 'what I said was quite true. If it weren't for Gil you'd be confronting me on a mortuary slab this morning. Please don't argue with him. You should be very grateful to him.'

Edward's nostrils flared with an indecipherable emotion as he said reluctantly, 'Then if I must accept Eleanor's version of events, may I offer you my thanks?'

'You're welcome!' responded Gil cheerfully. 'It was a pleasure saving such a beautiful young woman...' There was a decided glitter in his eye as he said that.

Edward looked at him suspiciously. He couldn't let the comment pass unremarked, but it was clear he had no desire to agree with Gil over anything—least of all his fiancée's virtues. 'Yes,' he said at length, 'Eleanor is certainly a very nice-looking girl.'

'Come, come,' cajoled Gil. 'The whole village has been agog since she arrived. Haven't you ever told her that she's beautiful?'

'Of course——' blustered Edward.

'For goodness' sake!' cut in Eleanor hotly. 'I'd rather you didn't talk about me as if I were a piece of meat! I can't see what my appearance has to do with anything, anyway.'

'Well said, my dear!' exclaimed Edward, patting her on the back.

Gil merely smiled. An infuriatingly satisfied smile.

Eleanor busied herself buttering a slice of toast. This was turning out to be even more excruciating than yesterday—if such a thing were possible. She wished fervently that she had stuck to her guns and had refused to join Gil for breakfast. Edward was such a dear, but repartee had never been his strong suit. And just as well, she reflected. Having tasted Gil's razor-sharp tongue— metaphorically speaking—she could think of nothing

worse than marrying a man whose main delight seemed
to consist in discomfiting others.

'Ought you take quite so much butter, darling?' murmured Edward.

She looked down at the slice of thickly buttered toast.
Perhaps she had been rather greedy with the butter, but
it looked so delectable, so pale and creamy, and so
patently fresh, unlike the rigid yellow bricks that the
supermarket provided, that she hadn't been able to resist
it. She lifted her knife to scrape some of it off.

'Your concern for Eleanor's arteries is very touching,'
remarked Gil silkily. 'In fact, I couldn't help noticing
that you were more concerned for them than you were
for her reputation, when you first arrived.'

'What do you mean?' asked Edward, nervously. Like
Eleanor he seemed to be becoming increasingly aware
that he had met a formidable verbal adversary.

'Well, you commented on the fat content of her
breakfast before you thought to mention that you believed her to have been unfaithful to you. I think that's
nice. I think it shows a very proper degree of self-
lessness—putting her health before your own emotional
well-being.'

Edward sighed impatiently, then frowned. He seemed
to be at a loss for words.

'What you fail to understand,' said Eleanor haughtily,
anxious to relieve Edward's obvious embarrassment, 'is
that Edward didn't really believe that I'd been unfaithful to him. He couldn't have. We have too much
respect for each other for that, you see. A concept which
you probably find difficult to understand.'

'You mean you two don't sleep together?' quizzed Gil
ingenuously. 'How very charming and unusual in this
day and age.'

Edward seemed to have got back on course. 'On the contrary...' he rejoined, his face colouring. 'It's all the more appropriate in this day and age to save such intimacies for marriage. What with the current decline in moral standards and family life and so on.'

Gil's eyebrows shot up, and his hazel irises became ringed with white. 'You mean you're hoping to change society by your celibacy? How splendid!'

Eleanor almost choked on her bit of toast as she furiously quelled her unwelcome mirth. Honestly, Gil was outrageous!

Edward's face turned beetroot-red. 'No. Well, not exactly. It's just that if more people behaved nicely— well, the world would be a nicer place, wouldn't it?' he said in a voice hoarse with annoyance.

Gil nodded thoughtfully, as if trying to grasp some very deep and obscure idea. 'I think you've hit on something there, my dear chap. Yes. It's quite an idea. And you feel that sexual frustration makes people behave in a...well, in a much *nicer* manner, do you?'

'Don't be absurd!' cried Edward, his voice choked with mingled frustration and anger. 'Of course I don't. I just meant that if everyone were to adopt a higher moral code then all sorts of social problems could be eradicated at a stroke!'

'I see,' nodded Gil. 'So your celibacy is meant as a kind of example to other people? That's marvellous. Quite noble in its own way. But, of course, it can only work as a strategy if you publicise the fact... Now how do you go about——?'

'Oh, stop it, Gil,' burst out Eleanor. 'You're being very unkind. You know perfectly well what Edward means. I think we should drop the subject.'

Gil caught his lower lip between his even white teeth. It couldn't have been more obvious that he was suppressing a smile.

'Very well. If you wish...' he murmured. Edward heaved a sigh of palpable relief.

Eleanor bit into her toast in silence. Honey dripped off its edge and ran on to her finger. She licked it off unthinkingly, far too preoccupied with the problem of separating Edward and Gil before there was more verbal bloodshed to worry about table manners. It was going to be hard enough as it was, patching up Edward's wounded dignity.

Edward watched her licking her fingers for a brief moment, before nudging her disapprovingly.

She could understand that Edward was annoyed with her, and perhaps even stupidly jealous of Gil. But Gil's relentless teasing of Edward could only be attributed to his cynical and twisted nature. He was incapable of appreciating someone as basically decent and straightforward as dear Edward. The sooner she finished her breakfast and got the poor man out of here the better.

'You never told us what prompted you to visit our little village?' asked Gil conversationally, beaming at Edward. Eleanor was pleased to note that his voice had lost its earlier tormenting edge.

Edward turned to Eleanor. 'I was worried about you,' he explained. 'You didn't ring last night. You've been so punctual up until now—seven o'clock on the dot, just as you promised. I waited till eight, then rang your home. When I discovered you hadn't rung there either, I was most concerned.'

Gil nodded at the telephone. 'Would you like to ring your parents, Eleanor, and reassure them that you're safe and well?'

Eleanor flinched. The calls home had been at Edward's insistence, and she wished fervently now that she had stuck to her guns and refused to fall in with his ideas.

'It's all right, Gil. I really don't need to...' she murmured, looking hard at her plate.

'It's OK,' Edward said soothingly. 'When it got to about nine-thirty I decided you must be having an early night. I rang your parents and told them, so that they wouldn't worry.'

'Thanks,' smiled Eleanor.

Gil looked puzzled. 'But she hadn't rung. So why did you stop worrying?'

'Oh,' Edward smiled confidingly. 'I understand Eleanor, you see. She can be stubborn at times, and she wasn't keen on this idea of ringing at a regular time every day. She's supposed to ring home every day to say she's arrived safely at work, too, but she misses the odd day when she's in a recalcitrant mood. Don't you, darling?'

Eleanor winced, then frowned at him in exasperation. What Edward was saying was no more than the truth, but she hated it all being spelled out to Gil like that. Though Edward had mentioned it in front of friends before, and she'd never minded then...

Gil's brows arched sharply, then he dragged them down into a frown. 'But if you weren't really worried about her, then why did you come rushing down? It's a long way, after all.'

Eleanor bit her lip. It had been on the tip of her tongue to say that he had come to check on her. But it really was a very ungracious thought. Dear Edward was so very protective. She ought to be pleased that he loved her so much. It was only her silly stubbornness that made her resent it.

'I—er—well, of course...I wanted to be sure... One does worry even when one knows one oughtn't,' muttered Edward, then turned a severe gaze on Eleanor and added, 'Which brings me to the matter of the tent. You told me you were going to find a nice guest-house, or bed and breakfast with some good people...'

Eleanor sighed again. 'I'm sorry, Edward. Really I am. I only brought the tent as a precaution. But as it happens I couldn't find anywhere suitable.'

'But Mr Prosser at the farm told me that you hadn't even asked if you could lodge in the house. He said they often take in paying guests in the summer and you'd have been welcome...'

'I didn't realise that!' exclaimed Eleanor fiercely. 'Anyway, I'm fine in the tent, so why——?'

'Eleanor has been telling me that she's an experienced camper,' intruded Gil, chattily. 'Apparently she's been camping alone since her mid-teens. She's certainly chosen a wonderful site in the Prossers' orchard. She's within shouting distance of the house, but is completely secluded there, and sheltered by the trees from rough weather. I must say, I envy her waking up there every morning for a week or so. Especially at this time of year.'

He turned to look at Eleanor, who was frowning furiously, and then Edward, who was watching him in dismay, his mouth half open.

'Don't you think it's impressive...' Gil continued, admiringly '...that she enjoys such a simple pleasure? So many young women are empty-headed materialists. Unless they're roasting on a beach at some fashionable European resort in a designer bikini——'

'If we need your opinion then we'll ask for it,' snapped Edward rudely. He stretched out his arm and squeezed Eleanor's shoulder so tightly that she found herself

leaning sideways in her chair towards him. Oh, no...
This was deteriorating again. She got to her feet and
took her plate over to the sink, avoiding Gil's eye.
Honestly. What with Gil being so snide and Edward so
unnecessarily protective she was almost ready to scream.
Men! What was the matter with them?

Gil was apologising for intruding. 'Naturally, it's
Eleanor's business where she chooses to stay,' he said.
'It's just that I admire her so much for her wonderful
independence of spirit, and her generous impulse in
helping that poor student finish his degree, that I felt I
had to defend her.'

Edward bristled. 'I have to say that I think her professor has a lot to answer for, expecting a young girl to
take off into the wilderness to collect data for someone
who should have known better.'

'You mean the boy chose to break his leg?'

Edward sighed leadenly. 'No, I do not,' he muttered.
'But if he had this fieldwork to do then he should have
given up his rugby football until he'd done it. It can be
a very rough and nasty game.'

Gil winced nervously, then murmured softly, 'You're
in Wales now, old chap. I'd be careful about expressing
views like that around here.' Then he added, somewhat
hurriedly before Edward exploded, 'So you think scientific research should be left to the men, do you?'

'If it involves sleeping alone in the wilderness—especially if it means it's impossible to get an uninter-
rupted eight hours—then yes, I do think that he should
have asked a man,' replied Edward.

'It must have been very humiliating, having your own
offer turned down,' Gil responded sympathetically.

'I beg your pardon?'

'I'm sorry, but I'd assumed that you would have volunteered yourself, if only to take the place of poor Eleanor, as you have such strong views on the subject.'

'Ah... Well... I wasn't able to offer my services. I'm working, as it happens.'

'But so is Eleanor.'

'Yes, but she's using up part of her annual leave.'

'Ah. I didn't realise. You must be stuck in a job where you can't choose when to take your leave. A factory, is it? Where they shut down for the same fortnight every year?'

'Certainly not!' Edward was almost squealing now that Gil had started up the sardonic banter again. 'I'm a junior partner in a very good firm of solicitors in the City as it happens. I have a very generous leave allocation...'

'So why——?'

'Edward's work is very important. He has to be available for court appearances and so on,' butted in Eleanor. She might have known that Gil's claws wouldn't stay sheathed for long. 'He can't just take time off at the drop of a hat.'

Edward grinned triumphantly, as if he had just said something very clever.

Gil nodded sagely. Then he came over and laid his hand on Eleanor's shoulder. 'I didn't realise you needed your sleep so badly. Some medical condition, is it? You shouldn't be so brave... If the villagers had realised I'm sure they would have set up some kind of rota to help with the midnight collections. The people around here are awfully kind.'

'The villagers certainly seem to be,' said Eleanor tartly. 'It's just a shame that the same can't be said for everyone who lives in this area.' And she cast a long meaningful glance up at Gil. He, naturally, assumed an air of incomprehending innocence.

Eleanor felt his hand lying heavily on her shoulder through the thin cotton T-shirt. It almost seemed to be branding her skin. You'd think her body would have got the message after seeing how unmercifully cruel this man could be when he got his talons out. But it apparently still saw him as her life-saver, and was determined to erupt most uncomfortably every time he came near. She hadn't known it was possible to be so pricklingly aware of someone's proximity. Her nipples had tightened again. If only she had put on her navy sweatshirt instead of this flimsy T-shirt when she had returned to her tent earlier that morning...

She bent her head over the sink so that her hair swung forward to hide the flush which she could feel creeping up her face. She was horrified at the thought that Gil might notice the effect his nearness was having on her treacherous body, and even more horrified to think that Edward, too, might notice. She ducked, moving out from under Gil's hand. He leaned against the draining-board, just inches away from her. She could feel his breath sifting lightly through her hair.

She glanced across at Edward. His face was so pink, his innocent eyes so round and bright. A huge wave of compassion and shame washed over her. Compassion for poor Edward, who had travelled all this way to make sure she was all right. And shame at herself for finding her lively intelligence quicken to the beat of Gil's merciless tongue. Anger flared inside her, compounding the tangle of emotions.

Drying her hands hastily on her T-shirt, she swept across the room and tugged at Edward's sleeve. 'Come on!' she said. 'Breakfast is over. We're leaving.'

Edward, who had been helping himself to a slice of toast and honey, hurriedly crammed the remains into his mouth and got to his feet.

'You can't go,' said Gil in stentorian tones. He was still leaning against the draining-board, and his relaxed posture was at odds with the harshness of his voice.

'What do you mean?' flung back Eleanor.

'We had a deal, remember? You'd have breakfast and then I'd tell you about the favour you owe me.'

Edward's colour had heightened considerably, but the half-round of toast was taking its time being chewed and swallowed. He was effectively gagged.

Eleanor slumped. She might have known she wasn't going to be able to sweep out in style.

'Tell me about this favour, then. Let's get it over with,' she said with bitter resignation.

'I have to go away on business for a few days,' said Gil, his eyes narrowing. They gleamed predatorily beneath his lashes. His mouth was mobile with yet another suppressed smile. 'I'll be leaving later today. Lily Matthew who has the land next to mine usually keeps an eye on things for me if I need help. But she's on holiday herself at present. The Prossers are looking after her smallholding, and it would be too much for them to look after mine as well. So I've decided that you can.'

'What?'

'Didn't you hear me? Then let me repeat——'

'Of course I heard! I'm just astonished at your nerve. It's not so much a favour you're looking for as slave labour!'

'Rubbish! There's not that much to do. Anyway, a few days' hard work won't hurt you. A small price to pay for your life, wouldn't you say? This isn't a full-scale farm—there'll be plenty of time for you to do your collections, and manage a couple of hours on the beach, if you get yourself organised. It's only really the animals that will need seeing to...'

'But I don't know anything about animals!'

'Then now is the time to find out. I'll show you around, introduce you to the goats and——'

Edward had swallowed. 'You're out of your mind. I've never heard anything so preposterous in my life! Come along, Eleanor, you're coming with me!' and he grasped her forearm with a firmness that almost made her cry out with pain.

Eleanor dragged her arm free, her face burning and her eyes blazing. 'Leave me to sort this out myself, Edward!' she said angrily. Then she turned to Gil and said between clenched teeth, 'You're taking unfair advantage of the...the circumstances.'

'Of course I'm taking unfair advantage. I *have* to go away unexpectedly for a few days, and your arrival is certainly fortuitous as far as I'm concerned. But I don't think you should refuse, however unfair you may think I'm being. It would do your soul good to discharge this debt so nobly. Though, of course,' he added speculatively, 'you may not be free to choose that option. You may have to do what Edward says. After all, the two of you are engaged, and it mightn't be a good idea for you to set a precedent by disobeying him.'

Eleanor groaned. He had her over a barrel now. If she refused to look after the farm then she would be acting despicably. She did, after all, owe Gil a whacking great debt, even if it *was* rather callous of him to be exacting payment like this. And, on top of it, Edward would think that she'd refused because he wanted her to. And although she loved him she somehow didn't find that prospect very enticing.

She rolled her eyes. 'Lead me to the goats...' she said wearily.

Edward took her by the shoulders and glared at her. 'Over my dead body!' he roared.

'Edward, I don't think he's being particularly nice about all this. But I'll show you the cliffs where I would have met my death yesterday if it hadn't been for Gil. Frankly, I don't think I have much choice. And anyway, it might be fun. I always enjoy a challenge.'

'Ridiculous!' he shouted, his lips whitening with anger. 'He can't make you do this. You didn't ask to be saved, after all!'

Gil guffawed.

The absurdity of Edward's words suddenly struck Eleanor as outrageously funny, too. Was he seriously suggesting that it would have been better that she had died rather than look after the farm for a couple of days? Of course not. It was just one of those silly things that people said in anger, but knowing that didn't make it any the less funny. She started to laugh helplessly.

Edward shuddered with fury. She had forgotten how much he hated people to laugh at him. He turned on his heel and strode purposefully towards the door. 'I don't know what's got into you, Eleanor,' he said coldly. 'I knew it wasn't a good idea your coming away on your own like this. I'm not staying here to be insulted by you and that...that...man any longer. You can ring me at seven tonight to tell me that you've changed your mind, or the engagement's off!'

Eleanor stared in horrified silence as he stormed out of the door, across the yard and into his car. He crashed the gears, throwing it into reverse—something he never normally did—and then accelerated away out of the yard, the engine roaring.

She continued to stare at the open doorway for several minutes, in stunned disbelief. Gil's hand on her shoulder practically made her jump out of her skin. He spun her round to face him.

'You're not going to change your mind,' he said, as if it were a statement of fact. She looked into his eyes, which were almost amber as the sun, streaming in through the doorway, caught them in its glare.

'No,' she said flatly.

'And if you're not going to change your mind, then the engagement must be off.' He smiled broadly, then added, 'Which is excellent news, as it frees me to do something I've been rather wanting to do for a little while now...'

And while she continued to look at him in baffled dismay his face loomed closer to hers as he bent to accommodate the disparity in their heights until his lips brushed hers and he was kissing her. Her mind was completely numb. Everything was so unexpected—except the shuddering response of her body as his dry lips first nibbled gently at her mouth, and then crushed bruisingly against her full, moist lips.

She had guessed from the tingling heat that his slightest touch had evoked that to kiss him would unleash a furnace. She had underestimated it. She was melting. His tongue probed against her lips, then her teeth, until suddenly she was kissing him back, their mouths melding, their tongues entwined, their hands slipping purposefully behind each other's necks to tangle in their hair—to pull the other's head ever closer into the closest of all embraces.

Her finger stroked the silky duck's tail of hair against the skin of his neck. His hands came down to grip her shoulders before travelling caressingly over her back.

And all the while they kissed, hungrily, compellingly, as if they had been waiting a long, long age for this moment. His hand curled around her ribs, his thumb brushing the full curve of her breast through the cotton of her T-shirt. He seemed to pause fractionally, and then his hand moved again across her breast, this time more purposefully, so that his thumb swept across the proud peak of her nipple, teasing it into a yet harder fullness and drawing from it sweet stabs of excited pleasure.

It was only when she found her body pressing urgently against his, when she found herself moving against him in a way that was at once unfamiliar and yet oh, so achingly familiar, as if some atavistic memory from the generations that had gone before had been stirred into life, that she pulled sharply away. Kisses weren't supposed to be like that. She'd had several boyfriends before Edward, and they'd all kissed her. She'd always enjoyed it, but never before had she found herself pulsing with this urgent, ferocious desire that had made her behave so demandingly. Surely, kisses were supposed to be mild, rather innocuous affairs? They weren't supposed to lead into such deep and dangerous waters...

She didn't like him. Physically he had some kind of alarming effect on her body, but she didn't like him. And no matter how profoundly his kiss had aroused her, intimating so seductively pleasures yet to be known, she couldn't let it go on. She was trembling as she freed herself. She took a few steps backwards, her lips burning and moist, her skin warm and dry and crying out for the contact which had now been broken.

'You shouldn't have done that...' she said huskily.

He smiled lazily. 'Oh, yes, I should. And well you know it...' His eyebrows arched, and his eyes widened with delight as he looked into her uncertain face.

She took a step back from him, increasing the distance. 'That...that was very wrong,' she insisted. 'On both our parts.'

He tilted his head, surveying her steadily. Then he lifted his shoulders carelessly. 'It was only a kiss,' he said softly.

'No, it wasn't!' she exclaimed, dismayed and confused.

He gave a small, dry smile. 'No, it wasn't, was it?'

Eleanor swallowed hard. 'I thought you said you didn't want to...to...' But she tailed off miserably. She couldn't bring herself to repeat his words.

She had reminded him, none the less. He gave a low growl of recognition. 'Well, so I did!' he exclaimed. Then he added drily, 'I think I must have changed my mind...'

'Edward didn't mean it,' continued Eleanor, almost pleading now for him to say something that would wipe all meaning from the embrace to which she had given herself so eagerly.

'I don't suppose he did,' agreed Gil, pulling a wry face and shrugging.

Eleanor dropped her eyes wearily. What did she expect him to say, after all...? 'Sorry about that...my mistake...you and Edward make the perfect couple...wouldn't have done it for the world if only I'd stopped to think...'

He wasn't going to let her off the hook that lightly. And, anyway, there was no real reason why he should. She was responsible for her own actions when all was said and done. And she couldn't deny to herself that she had wanted him to go on and on kissing her like that...

She looked angrily back up at him—an anger mixed with mortification. Doors in her mind seemed to have been blown open, and were banging and crashing inside her head as if a gale were blowing in there.

'Come on, Eleanor...' he said in a soft voice. 'Don't be hard on yourself. You enjoyed it every bit as much as I did. Just forget it for a while. Though you may as well get used to the idea that you liked it, because I've got a sneaking suspicion we'll be doing it again, before long.'

'We won't!' she muttered fiercely.

His response was to let out a low, enticing chuckle.

She pressed her lips together and scowled. 'I thought you were the one who said I should be taken seriously!' she exclaimed.

'So I did,' he agreed. 'But only when you're being honest with yourself, Eleanor.' He smiled. 'Only then...'

There was a long silence while he surveyed her lazily, then he continued, 'But I can wait. So why don't we forget all about it for a while and I'll show you how to milk a goat...?'

CHAPTER FOUR

GIL scribbled notes for her in a firm, bold hand as he took her round the few outbuildings and fields, showing her the animals and explaining what had to be done. She was unbelievably angry with him—at his galling presumption in assuming she'd manage the farm, never mind the kiss. She had taken his advice about the kiss, and was trying hard to forget it completely. Mostly she was succeeding. She had managed to lock the recollection behind one of those doors in her mind, but every now and then a gust of defiance would blow it open fleetingly, and she would be faced with the remembrance of his hot mouth opening over hers, before she slammed the image away again.

She was more furious still with Edward for making such a silly fuss—but relieved, too. It was no good. She'd known before she came away that he wasn't right for her. He was stifling her, and if there was one thing Eleanor didn't need any more of in her life it was that sense of being suffocated by goodwill. Watching Gil spar with him had finally settled her feelings. She could see that he was a very worthy type. He was going to make someone a perfect husband. But it would have to be someone else. If the truth be known, fond though she was of him, she felt about as much real love for him as she did for the average house brick.

The anger she turned on herself was a more formless thing. Grey and watery and disconsolate, it washed over her, chiding her unkindly. What was the matter with her?

What was she doing with her life...and why? And why hadn't she realised a long time ago that her feelings for Edward had never had anything to do with real love? The answer to that question snaked into her mind, only to be swiftly evicted. It was a crude sexual attraction she felt where Gil was concerned. Nothing more. And even that was a temporary phenomenon—brought about by gratitude. Even so, had she loved Edward properly, then she would have been incapable of feeling anything at all for another man.

'You're not listening...' said Gil matter-of-factly.

'I am——' she began to protest, but he shook his head.

'You were daydreaming, Eleanor. Which is an excellent sign, but is not going to help Porky, here, when it comes to feeding-time. Now I'll go back over it all again...'

'I don't see the point,' she sighed. 'After all, you're writing it all down anyway.'

'Yes. But you can't learn animal husbandry from a book.' He paused and gave her a relaxed smile. He had reduced both herself and Edward to jelly, but his own composure seemed as assured as ever.

She eyed him balefully, but inwardly took his point and tried to concentrate.

'The goats are going to be the most difficult,' he said, leading her across the orchard where his two fine pigs were rootling happily in the grass.

'I've heard,' she said, mellowing a little, 'that goats are terribly stubborn.'

His brown face split into a wide smile. 'You've heard right. Actually, you may not find them too difficult, after all. You ought to be able to understand their psychological make-up straight away. You have so much in common!'

She stuck out her lower lip, and frowned hard. 'Rat,' she muttered under her breath, but his amusement was infectious, and she was getting too used to his teasing to take the things he said too much to heart. Her mouth twitched a little, and then resolved itself into a rueful smile. He cuffed her approvingly on the upper arm, then let his hand slide round to rest companionably on her shoulder.

She winced slightly. His touch made her feel so very uncomfortable, though she knew better than to protest. It was a perfectly ordinary, everyday sort of gesture, and probably if she'd been wearing something bulky instead of this thin T-shirt she wouldn't even have noticed it. Really, she had to admit that it was very nice ambling under the trees in the morning sun, with his arm resting comfortably against the back of her neck. None the less, her shoulders must have tensed perceptibly, because his hand suddenly grasped her shoulder firmly, and then dropped to his side.

'Sorry,' he said lightly. 'I was forgetting that you're not a very tactile sort of person.'

She smiled weakly, but something very akin to disappointment clenched into a hard knot in her stomach.

'You'll have to get tactile with the goats...' he said, thrusting his jaw forward and biting his top lip. His eyes were sparkling now. 'There are three of them—all nannies—and they're all in milk. The only trouble is...' he was positively chewing at his upper lip now, and his eyes glittered with suppressed mirth '...they've been milked already this morning. I doubt we'd get so much as a drop if we tried now. So I won't be able to show you how it's done.'

He drew in an audible, sharp breath, then swallowed hard. 'They *must* be milked twice a day, on the dot—

they'll get mastitis if they're not. But not to worry...
There's a very good book on the subject back at the
house. I'll put it out for you.'

'On mastitis?'

'No. On hand-milking goats,' he said, clearing his
throat rather too loudly.

He needn't treat her like a complete imbecile! She knew
perfectly well that he was laughing at the very idea of
her milking the goats. Well, he could laugh all he liked,
but he'd be laughing on the other side of his face when
he got back. It couldn't be that difficult, when all was
said and done. People had been doing it since time im-
memorial. It might take her a little while to get the hang
of it properly, but she'd manage it—there was absolutely
no question of that.

'Shall I save the milk?' she enquired breezily.

He shook his head, a little more composed now. 'No.
There's no need, and anyway it would mean my having
to teach you all the sterilising and handling procedures.
Just give the milk to the pigs. They'll think it's
Christmas!'

They clambered over a small stile. Gil went first, and
briefly held out his hand to steady her, then, remembering, withdrew it. She gave him a grateful smile,
although that silly niggle of disappointment had
reintroduced itself. It was nice that he had taken her re-
luctance to be touched into account so readily. He obviously took her seriously, even though it clearly wasn't
his own style. It was an unfamiliar feeling—strangely
exciting in a funny sort of way. It made her feel... She
struggled to pin down the light, airy sensation that swept
through her. It made her feel free. That was it. And yet
that in itself was puzzling.

She'd always been free, after all. Her parents, and then Edward, had made it plain that they wanted her to be happy—to make her own choices. When other girls had had to stay indoors, helping their mothers, Eleanor had been free to do as she pleased. Though, of course, it had been hard to find things to do with all that free time, especially as she wasn't allowed to play outdoors. She seemed to remember doing her homework extra-thoroughly and her violin and piano practice—both of which she wasn't very good at and didn't like much—to while away the long hours. Edward, too, insisted that she was free to do as she pleased. She remembered him telling her, quite soon after they had met, that she was free to decide to wait for sex until after their marriage. She'd been pleased when he had said that. Pleased and relieved, she remembered. But she hadn't felt free. Or at least not in this heady, liberating way. It was exactly how she felt when she woke up in her tent, or when she lay down on wet grass to watch the sky. But it wasn't a feeling she'd ever associated with other people before.

Back in the farmyard it was scorchingly hot, especially after walking in the cool shade of the trees which grew every few yards along the ancient hedgerows.

'Mmm...' sighed Eleanor. 'This weather is marvellous.'

Gil stretched, pushing his long arms high up into the air so that the powerful muscles of his shoulders tautened the cotton of his polo shirt.

'There's a garden on the other side of house. Let's go out there and have a nice glass of ice-cold wine,' he suggested languidly.

Eleanor was slightly taken aback. 'But I thought you were in a hurry to get away? And you won't be able to drive if you've had a drink, surely...?'

His face crumpled, and he groaned mildly. 'I almost forgot that I've got to go...' he sighed. 'But it's OK. I'm not in that much of a hurry. It's your company that does it to me, Eleanor! You make my brain go all soggy...'

'Huh!' she returned. 'If today's performance has been an example of your brain feeling soggy, I should hate to be around when it's on form!'

He patted her on the shoulder. 'Well done!' he muttered. 'You're getting the hang of proper conversation, at last.'

'Don't be so patronising,' she said scathingly, narrowing her grey eyes. But she couldn't help feeling pleased.

He laughed, then strode into the house, and led her through the french doors and into the garden, pausing only to fill two glasses with ice-cold Perrier and a dash of white wine. There was a terrace beyond the glass doors, in one corner of which stood a white wrought-iron table and chairs, shaded by the overhanging boughs of a cherry tree.

The garden stretched out in front of the terrace, which had been created from worn flagstones. It was splendidly large, and quite beautiful. Roses twined up the trunks of established trees, over little pergolas and up the walls. There were lots of other things beside roses, including a bank of fragrant buddleia, alive with dancing butterflies, but it was the roses which caught her eye and held her spellbound with their beauty. They were so big...so wild and rambling and heavy with bloom. She sat in the shade and sipped at her wine. This was heavenly—or would have been if only her mind would sit still, too.

She sighed. Edward had been made to seem such a pompous old fogey once Gil had started sharpening his claws on him. Eleanor frowned as she remembered Gil's unmerciful teasing, and then found herself grinning wickedly at the memory. What on earth was happening to her? Edward had only had her welfare at heart, for goodness' sake. It was really very unkind of her to be remembering his embarrassment with relish. Gil had a very cruel streak in him—there was no doubt about that. But still her lips curled into a delighted smile.

Once they were settled in the dappled shade, Eleanor commented, 'This is a lovely place. But surely, with only a handful of animals, you must run the farming side at a loss?'

'Don't you know that well brought up young ladies don't discuss money, religion or politics?' he replied with that familiar acerbic edge to his voice.

'Oh, well,' she said, tongue-in-cheek, 'then I've nothing to stop me. After all, you were telling me how badly I'd been brought up only this morning!' She ran her fingers through her dark hair, pushing it away from her face.

He narrowed his eyes and gave a wry smile of appreciation. 'Let's just say that I can afford to look on it as a home rather than an investment.'

'That's no way for a captain of industry to talk!' she reproved, sipping at her icy spritzer.

Gil gave her a long, assessing look. 'You seem to be cheering up,' he commented at length. Then his eyebrows curved quizzically. 'I think we'll end up having quite a bit of fun, won't we, Eleanor? You're not such a prude after all.'

She shook her hair back to curtain her cheeks, which had turned a tell-tale pink. 'I don't know what you mean,' she murmured primly.

'You do. I don't know why you choose to act so dumb most of the time. You're as sharp as you're beautiful, behind all those blushes, aren't you?'

There! He'd said it again. Did he really mean it, or was it just a gambit in one of his perpetual verbal games? A gambit designed to entice her into his bed? She wriggled in her seat. Even a passing thought like that seemed to have the power to arouse her. 'I don't play those sort of games,' she said coldly. 'I don't act dumb, and I don't think I like your idea of fun.'

'That's only because,' he said in a low voice, 'you've never played by my rules.'

'I don't know what you're talking about,' she said, her voice as freezing in temperature as she could make it.

'And I thought you just said you never played dumb. Oh, dear, Eleanor...' and at that point he let out a very hefty sigh '... this is obviously going to take longer than I thought. I hope I can manage to be patient.'

She didn't reply. Instead she sat very straight in her chair and watched the butterflies on the buddleia. She sat like that for a very, very long time. She was not going to break the silence this time. Every time she opened her mouth she seemed to put herself in the firing line. The ordinary teasing—the type where he implied she was a despicable, brainless idiot—was bad enough. But this...well, this flirtatious nonsense was much worse. Because it made her feel all churned-up and excited inside.

Eventually he sighed again, quite naturally this time, before shifting in his seat with an impatient air. 'Tell me, Eleanor. What made you want to study geology?'

She peered at him suspiciously, reluctant to answer until she had assessed the question.

He hit his forehead with the heel of his hand. 'Eleanor! For goodness' sake! It's a perfectly ordinary question!'

'Oh.'

'Well?'

'Well...' She struggled to find the words. It wasn't an easy thing to explain. 'The thing is, I've always...well, I've always loved the earth. Right from my earliest childhood. My family home in London—I was born there and I still live there—is in a suburb. There's a garden, of course. Not very big. And a park about half a mile down the road, with a little boating lake and a few bedraggled swans. Other than that I've always been surrounded by the concrete and tarmac hurly-burly of the city.'

He responded with an attentive silence, waiting for her to continue.

She gave a light, nostalgic laugh. 'When I was a little girl I used to walk with my head bent, studying the cracks in the pavement. Other children played games with the cracks—trying not to step on them, you know? But I used to watch them to see the moss and the weeds growing. I was fascinated by the power of life to generate itself from just that tiny bit of soil.' She turned her head, looking at the rich loam of the flowerbeds beside her. 'The soil in the garden at home has become a sort of grey dust, from all the traffic fumes and the lack of vegetation to feed it. It *hurts* me to see it.'

She glanced at him, wondering if she was boring him with all this. But he was gazing intently at her. He didn't seem to be bored. Or, at least, not yet.

'Go on...' he murmured.

'Well, this fascination with the cracks in the pavements was the start of my interest in geology. I wanted to know how the planet was formed—how it had come to be so rich and fertile. I became intrigued by the subject.' She went on to explain how she had become increasingly interested in soil fertility, becoming certain that if only one could discover enough then eventually it would be possible to make even the desert bloom. But first it was important to understand the rock formations beneath the soil, and how they had contributed to its composition. And then it ought to be possible to understand a good deal more about what made one piece of land so much more productive than another.

'Why didn't you go on and do research after you'd got your degree?' he asked.

'I was offered the chance...' she began, but cut herself short. 'One can't go on being a student forever.'

'And if you had gone on to do research, what aspect would you have chosen?'

She laughed. Now she really was going to start boring him! 'Soil erosion. Glamorous, isn't it?'

'You mean the way the earth gets worn away by use? That's why the roads around here are sunken between the hedgerows, isn't it?'

She nodded, still smiling. 'That's part of it. But mainly I'm interested in the way plants bind the soil together. When trees are chopped down and not replaced, for instance, rainfall can wash centuries of rich soil away into the rivers, leaving bare rock in some cases. It can be disastrous for the people who farm the land... for the planet itself. You take those small meadows of yours near the river. You can afford to leave them just as they've been for hundreds and hundreds of years. But suppose you wanted them cleared and drained for crops—suppose you were a poor subsistence farmer who had no choice... What I was hoping to develop was a simple system of planting which would bind soils prior to land clearance. It would need to be related to the structure of the rock beneath. In fact, the underlying rock structure in Wales is particularly significant...'

She looked up, certain that he would be laughing at her obsession with the idea of protecting mud from man. But he was leaning forward, his eyes betraying his intense concentration.

He plied her with questions about her interest, which she answered eagerly, struggling to put the technical concepts into layman's terms so that he could understand.

At last she glanced at her watch, astonished at how quickly the time had sped by. 'Oughtn't you be making a move?' she asked nervously. She didn't like the idea of his going.

He ran his fingers along his jaw to the tip of his angular chin. His eyes burned almost auburn, dark beneath his shadowed brows. 'Yes...' he agreed laconically.

And, while her heart thudded in mortified recognition of his deliberate misinterpretation of her words, he stretched, got to his feet and came to stand behind her. His fingers came to rest lightly on her shoulders, then began massaging her neck, either side of her nape, very, very gently.

'I didn't mean that sort of move,' she said, but the words came out in a muffled whisper as a heady wash of desire caught in her throat.

'I know,' he said in a low, controlled voice. His fingers increased their pressure.

'Then will you please stop touching me?' she pleaded faintly.

'No,' he murmured.

'*Please* do as I ask,' she sighed helplessly, looking down at her lap.

He paused slightly, as if assessing her request. 'No. If you want me to stop you can always get up and walk away. But I don't believe you mean what you say at all. I think you spend too much of your time saying exactly what you think you ought to say. After all, at some point you must have said yes to old What's-his-name, and it's hard to believe you could possibly have *meant* that. I think that your mouth and your mind live quite independent existences.'

Very astute, whispered that inner voice. She said nothing.

Then, keeping one hand on her shoulder, he came to stand in front of her. 'I think,' he said, 'it's about time you started living quite a different sort of independent existence, Eleanor...'

Then he bent low and kissed her forehead very, very gently. She was staring at the open collar of his polo shirt. The strong curves of his neck, the coarse curling hairs which lay beneath his collar-bones, the scent of his tanned skin cried out to her. She wanted to bury her face against his shoulder. Weakly, uncertain of how to resist, she turned her head to one side. He was unperturbed, simply letting his firm lips brush across her forehead to caress the sweep of her shining dark hair. She tried to keep her breathing even, tried not to notice that every nerve in her body was alert, waiting for him to draw her closer to him...

She forced her eyes to focus. A long tendril of un-tamed rambler rose swayed gently in the sunshine. She was staring hard at an unfurling rosebud. It was darkest red, velvet-soft—she let her gaze be drawn deep into its hidden heart. Moist with the freshness of all living things, the rose waited to open to the sun—to become replete, full-blown, mature.

Gil's hands had dropped to her waist. He lowered himself on to his heels, so that he sat back, his muscular thighs stretching the fabric of his trousers tight. With a single finger he touched her chin, turning her face to meet his. And then he tilted her head slightly forwards, and his hands moved one to each side of her head, and he drew her face towards his and began to kiss her. She tasted the sharp tang of wine on his lips before her mouth opened to his. Then she tasted only him. Gil. The maleness of him. The blood surged in her veins.

She wanted him to pull her to her feet, so that she could be crushed against him as they kissed. Leaning forward in her seat, their mouths moving in such delicate unison, she knew that she wanted much, much more. His fingers curled against her satin hair. She longed to feel those fingers move against her back, her spine, her hips. Just as she longed to hold him in return. But her hands were folded tensely in her lap, the one impris-oning the other. She could only tell him of her need with her parted lips, her warm, responsive mouth.

But if her senses had spoken to him, then he had not been listening. Because after a few moments he gently disengaged himself and stood up, dropping a last kiss on to the top of her head.

'You know, Eleanor,' he said drily, 'I really must make a move now. Will you stop these delaying tactics, please, or I shall be late...?' And with that he stretched again, and then turned towards the house. He paused only to look over his shoulder at her and say briskly, 'I'll go and pack now. You can make me a cup of tea...'

Eleanor wrinkled up her nose. She had been treated like a fool, yet again. He had been teasing her when he had kissed her; mocking her for using an everyday expression so carelessly; taking advantage of her naïveté. But he had been right. She had known exactly what he had meant. She could have stood up and walked away. But she hadn't. She was free to choose.

And just then, being kissed by him, looking at that rosebud, she almost had chosen. It was a good job, she thought wryly, that he had kept some distance between them when he kissed her. Because otherwise she might have gone and given herself away. He would have teased her mercilessly then, and she wasn't quite ready for that. The realisation annoyed her.

She didn't warm the pot, and made the tea before the water had come to a full boil, hoping it would be horrible. And then she felt guilty, because she knew she was really more annoyed with herself than she was with him.

When he appeared in the kitchen he was barely recognisable. He was clad in a suit of charcoal-grey, beautifully cut, the outfit completed by a matching waistcoat which accentuated the breadth of his chest, a crisp white shirt, and a sober navy and green silk tie.

'Help me with the links...' he said, dropping a pair of gold cuff-links on to the kitchen table, and stretching out his arms towards her. She felt quite shaky for a moment, as she looked at him, his square chin freshly shaved and gleaming, his thick, wavy brown hair combed sharply back from his high forehead, and his hands held out towards her. There was something almost symbolic in his posture.

She swallowed nervously, and advanced towards him, picking up the cuff-links. They were astonishingly heavy. You didn't have to be a geologist to know that they must be solid gold. She wove them through the stiff button-holes in the starched shirt, taking care not to let her fingers brush against the backs of his hands or the hard knob of his wrist-bone. By the time she had finished her mouth was dry, and her breasts were starting to tingle with a fresh wave of desire.

'There...' she sighed at last, stepping back cagily.

His hands dropped to his side, and he surveyed her for a long minute through his green-flecked eyes. Then he took a mug of tea from the counter, drank it quickly in spite of its heat, and, gathering up a soft leather hold-all from the doorway where he had abandoned it, he crossed the kitchen on his long legs and went out into the yard. She followed him as far as the doorway, stopping to lean against the door-frame and watching as he opened the big doors to one of the outbuildings.

He had gone into the black cave beyond the doors, but it wasn't until she heard an engine throb into life that it occurred to her that the building served as a garage, and he was starting a car. The gleaming, grace-fully curved bonnet of a bottle-green car emerged into the sunshine. Eleanor caught her breath. It was the most beautiful car she had ever seen in her life. It was an enormous vintage Rover, its lines gracefully curved in stark contrast to the sleek aerodynamic shape of its modern equivalent. The hood was down, and the matching green leather upholstery shone softly in the sun. He eased the car out into the yard, then got out and went to close the garage doors.

She took a few steps towards him. 'You're not going just yet, are you?'

'Why? Can't you bear to see me go?'

For once she didn't get cross at his mocking tones. 'But—I mean—I don't know——— You haven't told me what to do about the horses.'

'The horses will be OK out in the paddock. They'll miss their exercise, but it can't be helped.'

'I can exercise them, if you like.'

'You can ride? But I thought you'd always lived in a London suburb?'

'Yes. But I had lessons at a riding school.' Sunday afternoons, to be exact. Two-thirty to three-thirty. Until her mother had seen that little girl fall off and sprain her wrist. Eleanor's lessons had been stopped, but the injured child had gone on to become a riding-school instructor... 'I even won a couple of rosettes at gymkhanas. But that was years ago. I expect I'm very rusty. Perhaps you'd rather I didn't.'

He frowned, taking his time about replying. At length he shrugged and said, 'Decide for yourself. The tack's in the stables.'

'Don't go yet. I haven't asked you——'

'It's all right. I wrote practically everything down in the notebook. It's on the kitchen table. And I put the book on milking goats out on the desk in the study. Make yourself at home. I'll ring you later!' And with that he stepped up on to the running board, swung into the driver's seat and pulled away.

'When will you be back?' she called. But he had gone.

She scarcely had a chance to look up for the rest of the day. The animals had to be fed, and Jip—who turned out to be adorably affectionate—taken into the village for a walk, which she combined with a visit to the post office to dispatch her samples, complete with the covering letter.

'Looking forward to your meal tonight?' asked the bustling postmistress.

'Pardon? I...?'

'With Gil. He's booked a table at the Bryn Glas hotel. He said he was going to ask——'

'He's had to go away on business, as it happens. I'm looking after his animals for him.'

'Oh...' Gwen Jenkins blinked in surprise.

'Mrs Jenkins?' asked Eleanor, deciding to shelve her bewilderment for the time being. 'Er—do you have any lump sugar?'

'Behind the tinned fruit. Why——?'

'I want to get on the right side of a couple of horses,' she smiled, paying for the sugar and leaving the shop before Mrs Jenkins extracted any more information from her. Now why on earth had Gil booked a table for dinner when he knew perfectly well he wasn't going to be there to eat it?

CHAPTER FIVE

'ELEANOR?'

'Yes. Or at least I think so. I'm too tired to be sure.'

'Did you get your collection done on time?'

She nodded, forgetting that Gil couldn't see down the phone, then hurriedly collected her wits and muttered, 'Yes. Just about. No thanks to you, though. Your very few animals have a way of making an awful lot of work.'

He laughed. 'The goats, I take it, took a little longer than expected?'

She glanced at her watch. 'I have spent three and a half hours peering into their demonic eyes, trying to figure them out. And I have been kicked and butted for my pains. They certainly did take a little longer than I expected, but I've got a feeling that *you* gauged it just about right.'

'Aah... They're nasty pieces of work, those goats, aren't they?' His voice was alive with that scathing humour of his. Eleanor, rather surprisingly, found herself grinning in response.

'Hmm. I'll reserve my judgement on that one, if you don't mind. I rather got to like them in the end. But that might just have been because I realised that they were bound to win every battle if I didn't give in and show them some affection. To tell you the truth, I felt absolutely doomed, and I suspect I was just making the best of a bad job.'

He laughed again, with a good deal of warmth. 'But you *didn't* have to resort to the Prossers?'

She feigned offence. 'Don't sound so disappointed! I've become very used to the fact that you see me as some kind of incompetent imbecile. But I don't see myself that way, and I had no desire to have the Prossers view me like that, either. They're nice people. So far we seem to have established a relationship based on mutual respect. I'd like to keep it that way, if you don't mind.' She dropped the pretence of being insulted, and added ruefully, 'Anyway, I was damned if I was going to let myself be thwarted by a trio of ill-tempered goats! I have my pride, you know.'

'Eleanor, you are extraordinary...' he said drily. She could imagine his tongue pressed firmly into his cheek as he spoke.

She groaned out her response. 'Don't try flattery again, Gil. It won't work. You've landed me with a load of trouble, no doubt hoping I'll fall flat on my face. Well, so far I've avoided giving you that pleasure. But if you think you can boost me up with compliments, so that I've further to fall when the time comes——'

'OK, OK. I get the point.' Then he asked, his voice cynical, 'Did you ring Edward, after all?'

'Naturally I didn't manage to ring him at seven. You and your goats saw to that.'

'And he hasn't rung you?'

'I don't know. I've been out of the house for rather an unexpectedly long while.'

'Excellent.'

'And just why should you be so pleased?'

'Because it means I can kiss you again when I get back.'

'Fat chance!' But even as she said it she was overcome by a wave of exhilaration.

She was feeling very tired and very relaxed. She had slumped back in the Windsor chair, and had propped her feet up on the rail at the side of the Aga. She didn't feel so threatened by him on the phone as she did in the flesh. His physical presence overpowered her, she had to admit, but the disembodied voice was a good deal easier to manage.

'Oh, come now, Eleanor. You'll enjoy it. Just like last time.' His voice was low and gravelly and very sensual.

She sensed the hair on the back of her neck prickling in reply. It alarmed her. She really wasn't ready to play games with a man like Gil. 'I . . . I shan't give myself the chance to find out.'

'Now that's called cutting off your nose to spite your face.'

Quite right, muttered a little inner voice. She ignored it. Oh, damn the man. Why was he so horribly sure of himself? Her mouth might be denying him, but her emotions weren't. She felt warm and excited at the idea of his coming back and kissing her again, and she didn't want to feel that way. She wanted to be in control of her own life. Not manipulated and twisted by someone who was a good many steps ahead of her in his plan to have what he called a little 'fun' with her. Was she never going to free herself from other people's machinations? She hated her body for responding so positively to him, when her mind knew perfectly well that he thought her a fool. A pretty fool, though, which, apparently, was quite sufficient as far as he was concerned. She said the first thing that came into her head.

'As it happens, I shall ring Edward just as soon as you clear the line. He's upset, but I'll soon win him round.' Her voice was starchy and determined.

'And that's called cutting off your head to spite your neck...'

'I really don't know what you mean!'

'All right. Then I'll spell it out.' He sounded decidedly harsh—as he had when she'd refused to admit she'd come close to drowning. 'Why do you need to win him round when he's the one who's behaved badly?'

She must have been mad to imagine that he made her feel *free*. She didn't want to ring Edward, of course. But he wasn't to know that. He was trying to impose his will on her again, and she didn't like it.

'You weren't too impressed by *my* behaviour either last night, if I remember. We're all of us capable of——'

'You're evading the issue again.'

She straightened up in the chair, feeling a searing stab of anger run through her. Why on earth had she got into this conversation in the first place? Whatever the reason, he was going to discover she was quite capable of making her own choices. 'I love him,' she said fiercely. 'Not that you'd understand something like that. I shouldn't think you have the first idea what the word means! But for me it means that I'm prepared to learn to live with his faults. I'm not interested in scoring points as far as Edward's concerned, because I... Well, because I love him.'

'Really?' His voice was very low—almost insinuatingly smooth.

'Yes, I do!' she lied loudly, standing up as if to emphasise the point.

'It seems to me,' said Gil acerbically, 'that your relationship with Edward has a good deal in common with your relationship with the goats. Speaking of which, don't milk them till half-past seven tomorrow. That's

their usual time. They don't like being out of routine.
It makes them very bad-tempered.'

'Then why,' she cried, tears of frustration springing
to her eyes, 'did you tell me to milk them at half-past
six tonight?'

'Did I? How foolish of me. I can't have been concentrating when I wrote it down.'

She gave an inarticulate hiss of exasperation.

'You sound tired,' said Gil brusquely. 'Have an early
night. Oh, and Eleanor?'

'Yes?'

'Sweet dreams.'

Later, when she tried to ring her parents, she found
that the phone wouldn't work. Somehow, that devious
rat had tied up the line.

It must have acted like an order on her brain. It was the
only explanation. After all, they were the very last words
she'd heard anyone speak before she finally went to bed.
And he did have this extraordinary sexual effect on her
at the best of times. At any rate, she'd never had dreams
like it in her life before. And they certainly seemed de-
lectably sweet when she was having them. It was only
when they woke her and she found herself trembling and
moist with desire in his big brass bed that the pleasure
of them fled, and she sat alone in the darkness, per-
turbed beyond reason.

The room smelt of him. The sheets and pillowcases
were still crisp with laundry starch. But his clothes hung
in the wardrobe and filled the drawers, and everything
in the room was his—had been chosen by him, had been
touched by him, had been used by him. Even the radio
station which woke her at five-thirty had been selected
by him. She would sleep in another room the next night.

Her investigations of the accommodation on offer, however, made her change her mind fairly swiftly. There was the room Gil had used when she was sleeping off her shock, and three others, all very nicely furnished. It was the fourth spare bedroom which made her decide to go back to sleeping in her tent.

It was quite beautiful. Sumptuously decorated in pinks and creams and a soft lovat green, it was entirely feminine. Both the enormous bed and the high windows were swagged in chintz. The bed—all ruffled and frilled—had so many plump pillows and scatter cushions that any occupant would virtually have to sleep sitting up. And the ivory en-suite bathroom was unmistakably female, with a rosy shower curtain, matching towels and bowls of little pink soaps. The huge cream wardrobe was not empty. At one end hung a cluster of female clothes. There was even a chic little cocktail dress, strapless, with a boned bodice and a figure-hugging skirt. And the underwear she found in one of the drawers was positively indecent. Eleanor slid the drawer closed, her skin burning. This wasn't so much a bedroom as a boudoir. And whoever had left this stuff here was certainly intending to return. Thank goodness she'd done no more than kiss him. Eleanor felt shamefully used. Until he came back, she resolved, she would sleep in her very own tent.

She took Jip down to the shore with her to make her collection. There was a lively breeze that morning for the first time, and it whipped his rough black coat into little whorls. He bounded along beside her, alternately panting and wheezing. He was a dear, even if he was a bit past his prime. He stayed well clear of the sea, which was as rough-coated as himself this morning. He was obviously no old sea-dog, but a land-lubber through and through! Perhaps he, too, had gone down for the second time on some occasion in his youth. She threw him a sympathetic grin.

She was making herself some breakfast when the phone rang next.

'Hello?'

'Who is that speaking?' The voice was cultured, female, and sharp.

'Er—I'm looking after Mr Rhys's farm while he's away on business.'

'But he's not away on business,' returned the voice confidently and very coolly. 'I, of all people, would know if he was. Gil and I are very close.'

'I'm sorry, but I'm not in the habit of telling untruths. Can I take a message?' Eleanor's voice had become correspondingly cold.

'Tell him Sylvia rang. That's all.' And a sharp click indicated that the conversation was finished.

Eleanor looked crossly at the phone. What a rude woman. She and Gil must have some pretty vicious conversations between them. If they wasted time talking, that was. More likely they spent their time frolicking around on that huge mountain of pillows upstairs. Having fun.

The phone rang again. She picked it up and murmured in her sweetest tones, 'Is there anything more you'd like to say?'

'Eleanor?' It was Gil, sounding at his most unpleasantly curt.

'Oh...' She was flustered. 'Yes. I didn't expect it to be you.'

'Obviously. How's the weather?'

'Good grief! I didn't think you were the sort of person who used the telephone merely to talk about the weather.'

'Just answer me.' That was an order.

'Well . . . it's not very nice, actually. The animals seem to be fine, though Jip doesn't like——'

'I don't want to know about the animals. I'm quite capable of leaving them for a few days without having a nervous breakdown.'

The comment cut deep. She remembered the look on his face when Edward had revealed that she was expected to ring home daily to say she'd arrived at work safely.

She swallowed hard, then continued with as much politeness as she could muster, 'Oh, so what *would* you like to know?'

There was an impatient hiss, then he said harshly, 'There's a gale-warning out for our sea area. Force eight to nine, apparently, with even worse weather on the way. It could be quite nasty.'

'You don't need to tell me. The breeze is very strong. I've been out there in it several times already. In fact, I'm just off out again now.' Her voice was deceptively even and crisp.

'Still having trouble with the goats?' he asked scathingly.

'I'm sorry to disappoint you but I'm afraid they behaved beautifully this morning. Take heart. It may only be temporary. I may get butted again for my pains. But don't expect me to show you the bruises.' She said that very coolly. She didn't want him thinking he could come back and take up where he left off.

Could you hear people smile? Eleanor had the unnerving sensation that what she had said had pleased him somehow. At any rate, his voice, when he spoke again, was much less acerbic. 'No other problems?'

'Absolutely none, you'll be sorry to hear. Oh, except that a woman called Sylvia rang.'

'Damn.'

She heard him stop smiling.

'What did she say?'

'She said that I was a liar and she knew for a fact that you were here at the house. Or words to that effect,' responded Eleanor, aware that she was being stupidly bitchy.

'She said what?'

'Er—well, she said to tell you that she had called. And she was rather surprised that you had gone away on business without letting her know,' muttered Eleanor angrily, wondering why she didn't feel any better for having given him a sweeter version of the brief conversation.

There was a brief silence, then Gil muttered, 'If she rings back, tell her that I'll be getting in touch with her shortly. OK? Don't say anything more than that. Whatever you do, don't mention this business trip of mine.'

Eleanor was irritated. Why should she cover up for him when his girlfriends rang? 'Are you having an affair with Gwen Jenkins, too?' she asked sourly, picturing the busy little postmistress with her untidy grey hair and spectacles.

'What?'

'Well, I found myself covering up for you with her, as well. She seemed to think that you'd booked a table to take me for a meal in some fancy hotel.'

The smile was back in his voice—very broad, very amused. 'Did she really?' And then he laughed. And then he said, 'Well, well! Whatever can have given her that idea?' And then he laughed again and said, 'Behave yourself... I'll be in touch,' and put the phone down.

Eleanor felt quite sickened. He was the one who had insisted that she wasn't dumb. And yet he treated her as if she was very stupid indeed. Now why was he so amused that she'd found out about the meal? She didn't want to amuse him. She didn't want him to enjoy his life at her expense.

She had saddled the grey mare before she figured it out. Gil had been intending to ask her to come for a meal with him when he'd brought her to the house for breakfast. That was the favour she was to have done for him. But Edward had irritated him. He'd only asked her to tend the animals because he knew it would infuriate Edward. The realisation filled her with a cold anger. He hadn't asked her to look after his farm because he had any respect for her at all. He'd done it simply because he disliked Edward. Wining and dining her as a prelude to having 'fun' with her was what he'd really had in mind. Thank goodness she hadn't succumbed when he'd kissed her. And what a stupid fool she was for feeling such a thrill of excitement every time she spoke to him or looked at him or thought of him...

She spent the early part of the afternoon in her tent. It was nice there. It smelt good. From now on she would steer well clear of him. She zipped up the tent as she left with the comforting thought that she would be back there that evening, and could snuggle down in her sleeping-bag with her torch and a good book. Tonight, she promised herself, she really would sleep well.

By mid-afternoon it was becoming clear that the next few collections were going to be impossible from the beach. The tide was in, and the waves were crashing close to the bottom of the cliff path. The sea, which the pre-

vious day had resembled a mill-pond, was a foaming
grey waste, and waves were rearing impressively before
dropping their massive weight on the shore. The rocks
were almost obliterated by a white froth of angry water.
It would be impossible to get a good sample from the
cove while the sea was running so high. After sending
off one batch with an apologetic note, she was anxious
that the rest of her samples should be as trustworthy as
possible. Never mind, she told herself equably, aban-
doning the tiny strip of spray-drenched beach and
making her way up the path. There was always Plan B...

She reluctantly trailed back to Gil's to see to the animals. She wouldn't go into the house, though, she decided as she made her way into the yard. She didn't want
to be around if the phone rang again. Her next thought
was that the car looked very different with the hood up.
Just as beautiful, but more imposing—less jaunty—
somehow. The following thought came in the form of a
severe reprimand. It was *not* a good thing that he had
come back so soon. She did *not* want to see him. Least
of all did she want to be kissed by him again, so she
could just put *that* silly little idea right out of her head.
Now.

She needn't have wasted the effort of convincing
herself. When he appeared from the stables, his waistcoat
unbuttoned, his jacket discarded and his shirt-sleeves
rolled back to reveal his bronzed, muscular forearms, it
was immediately apparent that the last thing he wanted
to do with her was to seduce her.

He glared at her, his face set in hard lines. He was
holding a bridle in his hand.

'Where the hell have you been?' he snarled.

She looked at him in aggrieved surprise. 'I've been in
my tent. Why? What business is it of yours?'

His response was to hurl the bridle at her feet. The leather whipped the air, and the metal of the bit drew a spark from the cobblestones, so hard had he thrown it.

'Your tent may not be my business, but *that* most certainly is, you little fool!' he roared, indicating with disgust the bridle at her feet.

She looked at it in dismay. She knew she should have finished cleaning the tack earlier, but she'd been in a rush to do her collection. She remembered from her riding-school days how important it was to look after such things properly. Even so, his reaction was quite excessive. He really could be very nasty when he was in a bad mood. 'I'm sorry,' she murmured with a distant politeness. 'I meant to clean it earlier...'

'Damn it, Eleanor!' His teeth were clenched, and his eyes flashed with anger. 'You've got about as much sense as a plucked chicken.'

'I don't see why you should be so annoyed with me,' she countered valiantly. 'After all, you said it was up to me whether or not I exercised the horses. Don't take it out on me just because I chose to take them for a canter!'

He seemed to struggle to bring his anger under control at that point. The hard line of his mouth eased a bit, and he dug his hands into the pockets of his trousers. 'I was assuming that you knew how to exercise discretion, as well as horses. Obviously I overestimated you.'

She looked into his condemning eyes and then back down at the bridle. Light dawned.

'That's the gelding's bridle,' she said uncertainly.

He gave her a look of cold disdain. 'Well done. And that's the sky and that's the house and that's——'

'You think I rode him?'

'I certainly think you did.'

'Well, I didn't.'

'Really? Then I'm just imagining the froth on the bit, am I? You've been nowhere near the horses. You know nothing at all about it. Somebody else must have taken the gelding out for a hard gallop. I can't imagine why you're bothering to lie. It's your neck I'm thinking of, Eleanor. Lies aren't going to save it from getting broken.'

Eleanor's blood had frozen in her veins. There was a horrible, leaden feeling in the pit of her stomach. 'I'm not lying! How dare you——?'

'You don't tell lies, do you, Eleanor? Only the truth will do for someone as perfectly upright as you.'

Her face coloured. She had lied to him about loving Edward... Only because he seemed to think... But even so. 'No. I don't lie ... or, at least, not usually, but you see——'

'Congratulations for being so honest.'

'No, Gil. You don't understand. Listen——'

But he didn't stay to listen. He had turned coldly on his heel and was striding into the house.

Eleanor turned just as briskly and made her way back to her tent. Damn him and blast him. She couldn't imagine why she should be crying. Well, not crying exactly. Just sniffing now and again. Well, he was back now, and he could milk his own stupid goats. And serve him right if they took a bite out of that immaculate suit of his. Right in the seat of the trousers. She was here to collect samples of sea-water, not to waste her time arguing with some erratic, filthy-tempered beast of a man.

She had worked out an alternative way of collecting samples when she had first arrived in case the sea turned rough. She would try it out at six, and if it worked well she could use the method until the seas had become calmer again. She fetched all the equipment she would need from the back of her car and then set off for the cliff-top.

Once finished she hurried back to her tent to don a warmer jumper. It wasn't quite as cosy there as she had imagined it would be. The wind was howling itself into a frenzy. The fly-sheet flapped like a sail, and every now and then the wind would find its way into the tent and send the sides ballooning outwards. The trees in the orchard creaked and groaned. They were sturdy fruit trees—not huge oaks and elms. But she still didn't relish the idea of one coming down on her tent. Calmly, remembering her training, she set about packing her belongings into her rucksack. The tent was far more likely to capsize than a tree was to fall and she didn't welcome the idea of her underwear being scattered to the four corners of Trenawr. She could sleep in the Prossers' house tonight. They had said from the outset that she was welcome if the weather broke.

She was just setting off to the house when Gil appeared. Judging by the expression on his face, his mood hadn't changed at all. But the suit had been replaced by jeans and a sweatshirt. He caught hold of her arm, his fingers digging hard through the quilting of her cerise anorak. 'Come on,' he said wearily. 'You're coming back with me.'

'Why? Have you discovered any other little jobs I've left half done? Have you managed to completely misconstrue the so-called "evidence" yet again? Are you planning to set me detention as a punishment for my wilful ways, or do you simply intend standing over me until I've cleaned up properly?'

'Your rather childish assumptions about how people react when they're annoyed says a lot about your character, Eleanor.'

She looked at him in disgust. 'So I'm to be treated to another dose of your unwelcome and uninformed comments on my nature, am I?'

'Grow up, Eleanor,' he muttered disdainfully, his eyes narrowing coldly.

'Let go of me!' she protested, trying to shake her arm free. Even through the bulky clothing her body was pulsing in response to his touch, and the realisation infuriated her.

His reaction was to lock his fingers even tighter on her arm, so that she had to struggle not to cry out with pain. 'No chance. You're coming back with me.'

'This is crazy. Why should I do what you say?'

'Because you need looking after, that's why.'

She turned fierce grey eyes on him. 'Hypocrite! You mocked my family for being over-protective, and now you're behaving in just the same way. Only worse. At least they know that I'm honest. And at least they behave that way because they love me. Whereas you just like pushing people around. Why can't you accept that I'm quite capable of looking after myself?'

'Because you're not! If you want to be treated like an adult, you'd better start behaving like one.'

She looked straight at him. 'You said you approved of my camping,' she muttered scathingly. 'But you didn't mean it, obviously. It was merely said in the hope that it would produce the desired effect. You want to watch out, Gil, or you may find *your* mouth and *your* mind living quite independent existences!'

'I did approve of your camping. But that was before this weather blew up. And before I realised that you were born without an ounce of common sense. No wonder your parents insist you ring to say you've arrived safely at work. I wouldn't trust you to the end of the street, let alone on a bus journey across London.'

She struggled then and began lashing out at him. What was it about her? Why did she endlessly attract this sort of nannyish behaviour? She had thought Gil was different! Well, he certainly was. He was a bully and a hypocrite. Suddenly she hated him.

With the force of one hand alone he held her at arm's length. He seemed quite unperturbed as her arms flailed and her legs swung helplessly in his direction. 'Tantrums won't help matters, Eleanor.' A skin of frost coated his words.

She pulled herself together then, and stood still, looking at him with hot fury burning out of her grey eyes. She would have loved to kick his shins so damned hard that right now he would be hopping around, squealing. But he was far too strong for her. If she had gone on fighting him she would only have made an even bigger fool of herself.

'If you must know,' she said in a voice which shook with emotion, 'I was just off to the house to take up the Prossers' offer of a bed for the night!'

He looked at her disbelievingly for a moment, and then, his lip curling with distaste, he let go of her so abruptly that she stumbled and almost fell to the ground.

'Go away!' she said, nearly choking on her anger. 'Go away and leave me alone. Permanently.' The wind whipped a strand of her long dark hair across her face, stinging her eyes. She screwed up her face and ducked her head out of the wind while she rubbed her eyes.

'Don't bother to come back. Ever. I never want to see you again for as long as I live!' she continued, pushing her hair back from her face and turning towards him. She had been speaking to thin air. He had already gone.

She rubbed almost frenetically at the top of her arm, trying to get rid of the burning imprint of his fingers. He was right about one thing, though, she conceded. She must be pathetically immature if she allowed herself to care one jot about anything he said or did. But she would soon knock that little aberration into shape. She was taking full control of her own life, beginning right now.

Determinedly she crossed the yard and knocked on the Prossers' door. No reply. She'd forgotten that they'd said they would be out for the evening—till eleven-thirty or so. She hastily scribbled a note and pushed it through their door. Then she moved her car into a safe, sheltered spot beside the barn and settled down to wait out the hours till midnight. It would be too late to knock up the Prossers when she got back, assuming she didn't manage to see them before she went. Never mind. She'd even go back to Gil's if she really had to, loathsome though the idea might be. Her safety was more important than her pride on a night like this, and she damn well wasn't afraid of him now, nor of anything else he might say. She was in charge of her own life and that was that.

She must have dozed, because when she opened her eyes it was dark. The farmyard was surprisingly full of bustle. Rain was lashing almost horizontally, and she could hear the wind moaning out at sea. It took her a while to make any sense of the black shadows, hunched against the wind, which moved swiftly across the yard. Two Land Rovers were parked near the orchard gates, their headlamps illuminating the rattling trees. Faint voices could be heard, buffeted into intelligibility by the screaming air. Mrs Prosser, well wrapped up against the weather, scurried across the farmyard to the orchard. Eleanor was pleased to register that she had her note in her hand. At least they wouldn't be worrying unnecessarily about her in the midst of all this commotion.

What was going on? She could make out a couple of shadowy figures in the orchard. Ah! Now she could see. A tree had come down, after all. Judging by the fuss, a sheep had been trapped by the fall. They often strayed into the orchard. One of the figures roared something into the teeth of the gale, then stooped and—good lord, whoever it was must be incredibly strong!—actually lifted the tree with his bare hands and moved it aside.

Anxiously she glanced at the luminous dial of her watch. It was no good, sorry though she was for the poor sheep, and much as she would like to offer her help—the midnight collection was due. She really couldn't wait. She zipped herself into her waterproofs, and with a powerful flashlight in one hand, and her pack of equipment slung over the other shoulder, set off. She tried not to admit to herself that she was frightened. Storms didn't seem to have quite this magnitude in a London suburb, with the streetlights standing steadfast on their concrete stems, the manicured lawns impervious. Here trees bowed towards the earth, while entire hay fields prostrated themselves before their master the wind.

She was lying near the cliff-edge, the collection completed, the plastic bottle containing her sample in her pocket. Her flashlight lay beside her on the drenched grass, sending its beam over the precipice to where the water boiled and fermented far below. The noise of the sea was awesome. It obliterated the moaning wind and the mad rustle of wet leaves and branches. Eleanor's heart pounded in response to the terrible, deathly roar. She pressed her ear to the wet earth, feeling the sound vibrate against her cheek, closing her eyes against the eternal rain-soaked blackness of the night. And then, with a cry of pain and shock, she felt something very heavy crashing down upon her body, pinning her hard against the cold, wet ground.

CHAPTER SIX

FOR a moment Eleanor thought she had been winded because it was so hard to breathe. But with relief she realised that it was simply the weight on her ribs that made it difficult to draw air into her lungs. Tentatively she acknowledged that she didn't seem to be in any pain, so she couldn't have been injured. She mustn't give in to the panic which danced at the periphery of her mind, or she would stand no chance of helping herself. She must work things out. What had happened? The hawthorn tree was too far away to have come down on her, and anyway, in this wind, it would have fallen the other way...

The noise of the sea crashing on the rocks below and the howling rage of the wind filled her ears so that it was some moments before she realised that somewhere—she couldn't have said where—she could hear a human voice. She hiccuped out a sob of relief. 'Over here!' she cried feebly, disappointed by the faintness of her voice against the cry of the storm. She felt stupefied by the strangeness ... the blackness ... the fear ...

Then suddenly she wasn't dazed at all, but fully alert and horribly conscious that whatever had come crashing down upon her with such force was alive and warm and sliding back off her and gripping her hard and pulling her backwards, away from the cliff-path and towards the field. She had moved several feet, her face dragging uncomfortably against the wet grass, before she managed to let out a great roar of protest.

Her assailant stopped, slackening the invincible hold. She rolled over on to her back, only to be blinded by a powerful torch turned directly on her face.

'Stop it!' she shouted, trying to make her voice heard above the storm.

In response the beam was tilted downwards, away from her face and on to her orange jacket. In the thin pool of light it created she could make out the face of a man, kneeling at her side, the eyes bright and hard as gemstones as they caught the light.

'Gil! For crying out loud!' She dropped her head back on to the grass, trembling uncontrollably. She didn't know whether it was fear or relief which had gusted into her mind—and she was way past caring anyway.

'Eleanor?' He said something more, but she couldn't catch his words in the roar of the storm. She put her hands over her face, pressing her fingertips against her eyes in a primitive attempt to stem the gouts of tears that were warming her cheeks. She was completely disorientated—her emotions were in a crazy turmoil, and the inky darkness and the lashing wind and rain compounded the effect so dramatically that she could make no sense of his alarming and forceful appearance here on the cliff-top. She was crying with the inexplicable spontaneity of infancy—not understanding whether there was even any emotion behind the tears.

She rubbed hard at her eyes, stopping the salty flow, and struggling to get some grip on reality. How had he got here? What was going on? Was he attacking her or trying to save her—and if so from what?

His arms were insinuating themselves under her, and he lifted her to her feet and pulled her yet further from the cliff-edge. She let herself rest limply against him, not knowing how to react, and simply surrendering her will to his until the confusion passed, letting her steps match his, and leaning heavily against his hard frame.

She was conscious that he was taking her through an open gateway, and into a field. She pulled sharply away from him as she felt the rope tighten against her harness, and realised that she was still attached to the tree. She fumbled to release the catches, her old training taking over. Only when you are sure you are safe, she remembered the instructor saying, should you release the harness. Obviously, if nothing else, she must feel safe, she registered with a dark irony.

She looked around for him. The beam of his torch was partly obliterated by the bulk of his body. He must have his back to her. With a shock she realised that the light was moving away from her. He was going. Her own torch was on the edge of the cliff. The darkness threatened. Suddenly awash with panic, she dropped her harness to the ground and began to run after him. 'Gil!' she cried. But the mocking wind blew the words back into her face. She ran after him, stumbling in the darkness, battered by the wind and rain. Again and again she cried out his name.

She caught him at last. 'What do you want?' he shouted angrily.

'Don't leave me, Gil...' The plea formed on her lips automatically, without thought.

'I should tell you to go to hell!' he jeered, but he none the less swept her up in his arms and positively sprinted across the field towards two points of light. It was his Land Rover, its headlamps blazing. He threw her into the passenger-seat then crossed to the driver's side in a few long strides, sprang up behind the wheel and roared off.

The short journey to the farm passed in silence. It was pitch-black inside the vehicle, though the powerful headlights lit up the narrow lanes, sunken between the high hedgerows which shivered and danced maniacally in the wind. Eleanor turned to try and discern something of his expression, but the darkness obliterated his features and all she saw was the glint of his eye and the shade of his profile as he drove steadily onwards.

He almost dragged her from the cab and down on to the cobbles of the yard. His fingers bit into her arm through the thick protection of her waterproof jacket and the sweater beneath. Then he swung her round to face him and his mouth came down speedily, violently upon her own. He was kissing her not with the delicacy of the previous day, but with a hard and fierce urgency. The rain and the wind seemed to lash them together, so that their mouths instantly melded into a burning fire in the midst of the tempest. His tongue curled strongly against hers, exploring her mouth ruthlessly, as she yielded joyously to the pressure of the kiss.

She was kissing him back with a wild, wanton passion, matching his fervour with a need every bit as intense as his. As her mouth opened to him it felt as if her whole body were opening, too. It was formless. A sensitive, pulsing void that stretched into the blackness of the night, arching and aching with a potent, almost painful pleasure. Her mind was empty of everything except the passion of the moment. Her body and mind were one— continuous not only with each other, but with him, with his soul . . . and with the night beyond.

Inside a great tidal wash of desire swept through her and over her and around her, turning to a hungry, compelling need that speared her quickly and demandingly in that deep, hidden place. Within moments she was aroused as she had never been aroused before. Urged by instinct, her tongue darted out to lick at the rain which ran down his face.

His arms were behind her, clasping her, then releasing her to tear at the zip of her jacket, while she clung desperately to him, anxious not to be parted by so much as a hair's breadth from the firm, muscular strength of his body. Her fingers dug through the drenched wool of his jersey, almost clawing at him in their need to find his flesh. Her hands slipped up beneath the ribbing of the sweater. She tugged insistently at his shirt until she found the silken skin of his back, tautly stretched over iron muscle and hard bone, spread sensuously beneath her curling fingers.

His hand found her breast through her sweater, squeezing and tugging at the hard, proud nipple, while a desperate groan escaped from his throat. She could feel, suddenly, his hard arousal pressing through layers of stiff, wet denim, and she found that she, too, was gasping, whimpering, moaning with an extraordinary elation. His hand now had found its way to her flesh, cupping her breast softly for a moment before the fingers tightened and his thumb thrust urgently against her nipple, drawing from it fresh torrents of spiked delight.

They were together, held close, moving, stroking, kissing, biting while the wind took all sound from them and the rain ran rivers over them, cascading from their hair into their eyes, blurring all vision so that there was only raw sensation...only the primal, elemental sensation of profound human need turning flesh to fire.

And then, when Eleanor felt that she could bear not one second more, when she felt that this roaring, consuming hunger must be assuaged, he gathered her into his arms and took her into the dark stables and laid her

tenderly on a huge bed of hay. The rain could not reach
them here, but the wind still gusted in, whipping against
Eleanor's damp flesh as he thrust her jacket from her
and pushed at the clinging mass of her sweater to reveal
her breasts. His mouth came down hard on her proud,
swollen nipples, drawing them deep into his mouth, while
the rough barb of his chin coursed against her soft skin.
Her hands pushed urgently at his clothing, baring his
hair-roughened chest to lie sweetly against her face.

She was crying aloud the demands of her roused body,
her voice weak against the crash of the storm raging
outside. His thigh lay heavily across her own, pressing
hard against her mounting need. Soon...soon...she
could not wait. She could not deny him. Her body arched
to meet his. Bone ground hard against bone, while his
fingers plied her flesh with tormenting urgency.

And then suddenly light burned white against her eyes
as a harsh snap of lightning jumped from sky to earth.
There was a deafening crack of thunder, and the cloud-
ridden sky, outlined by the stable doorway, was, for seconds together, ablaze with searing light. He stiffened
in her arms, pulling back, and then he half dragged her
to her feet.

'For God's sake, move,' he growled.

She gasped, still craving him, her body unable to make
sense of the turn of events.

'Come on!' he urged. 'The storm's overhead. This
building is thatched!'

Finally grasping the necessity of moving quickly, she
sped, sheltered by his arms, to the kitchen door. One
hand disengaged itself, and fumbled mundanely in the
back pocket of his jeans for keys. The door opened and
she was pulled through into the still warmth of the house.

The thunder and lightning had broken the spell. Still throbbing with desire, her mind suddenly became saturated with the realisation that she had almost—had very nearly—and most certainly would have—made love with Gil.

She pulled apart from him, shocked and appalled. There in the kitchen with the lights blazing, and the door slammed shut by the wind, she stood back and watched him as he turned slowly to look at her. His face was as thunderous as the night beyond the walls. His eyes flashed green and amber fire as they took in her drenched form, her long hair plastered in dark streaks to her skin, which was pale beneath the tan. She surveyed the proud angle of his jaw, the implacable planes of his face, and wondered if he, too, was confronting her with the same appalled realisation clouding his mind.

His lips parted, and he ran his tongue experimentally over them, licking away raindrops. 'Well?' he asked roughly, his voice thick with desire, 'just where do we go from here?'

'Not to the bedroom, that's for sure...' said Eleanor in a low voice, shivering slightly.

He kept his fierce eyes fixed on her, 'Isn't it the obvious place to finish what we've begun?'

'As far as I'm concerned, it's already finished. In fact I'm sorry we started...'

'Really? That wasn't how it felt back there.' He paused, turning his dark eyes on her wet face. 'Why are you punishing yourself, Eleanor?' His voice was grindingly low, grazed with undischarged anger.

She dropped her gaze to the sodden tips of her boots. They were surrounded by a pool of rainwater which gleamed like blood on the glossy red quarry tiles. She trailed her foot through the puddle, drawing a shimmering tendril of water out to one side, like the tentacle of an octopus. 'I don't know what you mean,' she muttered.

'I mean that you want me as much as I want you. I don't think there's much point in either of us pretending otherwise, is there?'

'No,' she acknowledged huskily. 'I admit I'm physically very attracted to you. But it doesn't mean that I want to give in to that attraction.'

'Why?'

She hesitated. He had saved her life, stirring in her some primitive need to display her obligation to him. Mankind was tribal by nature, she told herself desperately. Buried beneath centuries of civilisation was a more intuitive, instinctive animal, who looked for leadership. Knowing that she owed him her life had raised these emotions from the dark depths of her unconscious mind. But it could only be fleeting, this return to instinct. Tomorrow or the next day or the next she would awake, and it would be gone. And she would have marked her soul for a chimera.

'Because I . . . don't like you. And you don't like me. It's not a very sound basis upon which to make love, is it?'

He didn't say anything. He just stared at her. And for once his expressive brows weren't giving anything away.

She looked deep into his dark eyes with her clear grey ones. But she couldn't hold his gaze. It was unbearable—like meeting the eye of a cat. She flinched slightly then dropped her eyes to the floor again.

He made a sharp, explosive sound of scorn, then said, 'You like me well enough, Eleanor. When you forget whatever it is you think you *ought* to be feeling—when you speak to me without weighing your words—you like me well enough then. But you won't allow yourself to follow your instincts, will you?'

'So *you* follow *your* instincts as far as I'm concerned, do you? You instinctively believe the worst of me at every turn. And yet you instinctively want to get me into your bed? So you instinctively choose not to give a damn about how I might feel about this instinctive behaviour of yours?'

He sighed heavily, glowering at her. 'I know that you... Oh, hell! Come to bed and I'll show you what I mean. You'll understand something then which is beyond words...'

'No!' The brief word carried all the pain and longing she felt welling up within her. If the lightning hadn't crackled, the thunder hadn't roared, she would have gone with him anywhere—gone in his arms to his bed, or lain in the sweet hay of the stable, and would have made love with him without once thinking. But the spell had been broken. The thoughts had tumbled free, and there could be no going back.

'Why not? It can't be because of him? You can't really believe that he loves you?'

'Can't I?' she cried, lifting her chin challengingly to view him. All she knew was that she must keep on resisting Gil. With a heavy irony she remembered him telling Edward that he should take her seriously. Her heart had lifted then. It was as if a huge bubble of hope had swelled inside her at those words. And yet since then he had done nothing which could be construed as taking her seriously. The bubble had burst. Grimly she watched him. His hair was darkly wet, a lock falling in a heavy wave across his high, sunburned forehead. Rainwater beaded him from head to toe, so that he seemed to

sparkle beneath the harsh electric light. He is beautiful,
she thought, dangerously.

'But you don't love him!' Gil persisted. 'You can't!
You don't know the meaning of the word yet. And you're
determined not to let yourself find out...'

'I do!' she protested, adding, 'There's more than one
kind of love!'

He shook his head. 'No. There's only one kind. The
kind that sets your heart free. That has it singing like a
bird with happiness. The kind of love that *you* feel for
places, Eleanor. For rocks. For the earth. Only better.
Because when you offer love to a person that love be-
comes complete. It answers back... It's there for taking
as well as giving... Come back into my arms, Eleanor,
and let me show you.'

He peeled off his wet jersey. His shirt, still hanging
free from the waistband of his jeans at the back, clung
to his skin.

'Show me? Show me...love? You don't seriously
expect me to believe that you love me!'

'I want to make love with you, Eleanor. I want to
hold you in my arms and make love to you very much.
I want you to know how it can feel...' He was unbut-
toning his wet shirt.

She looked away. She didn't want to see his chest, those
dark curling hairs, the muscular arms. She didn't want
to be here. She didn't want to be having this conversation with this man. She wanted the past days to be
miraculously wiped away. She wanted to be lying in her
tent, waiting for a glorious dawn, and happy with the
moment.

He eased his feet out of his rain-blackened shoes, and
peeled off his socks. He was wearing nothing but his wet

jeans, which clung to his hard form, outlining the
muscles of his buttocks and legs.

'I know what you mean, Eleanor,' he said sourly. 'You
want me to say that I love you with all my heart, and
I'm planning to go on feeling like that forever. In other
words you want me to rubber-stamp your decision, to
package it up in convention. To make it safe. Well, I
can't do that. You like taking risks—but not where your
emotions are concerned. I'll bet that tame toad of yours
says all the right things, doesn't he, Eleanor? But he
doesn't make love to you. And if he did it wouldn't feel
the way it did just then, out there in the storm. The only
promise I can offer you is that if we made love it would
be something very special indeed. Can he promise you
that?'

'No...' she whispered, but she looked away as she
said it. He was good with words. It didn't alter the fact
that he despised her. He used her.

There was a silence and then Gil said quizzically,
'You're not wearing his ring.'

'No,' she agreed a little more evenly. 'I'm not. Things
are quite finished between Edward and me. You were
right. I don't love him.'

'Last night you told me in no uncertain terms that you
were prepared to put up with his overbearing smugness
for the rest of your days in the name of true love.'

'I told you that because I was frightened that if you
kissed me again I'd make love with you. I've already
admitted that I find you extremely attractive.'

'So what's changed? Why are you telling the truth
now? Because I caught you out in yet another lie?
Because I spotted that you weren't wearing his ring?'

'No. I could easily have said that I'd just taken it off
temporarily. I told you the truth because the lie was

serving no purpose. It hasn't, in other words, stopped you from trying to persuade me into your bed.'

'You lie very readily, don't you?' he said coldly. 'Just as you lied earlier this evening.'

'I didn't ride the gelding. I've told you that. You can choose to believe me or not. I don't care. I've no intention of arguing the point.'

'I didn't mean that, as it happens. At the Prossers', earlier, you told me that you'd arranged to sleep in the house. I would never have left you there in that storm if I hadn't believed it was the truth.'

'It was the truth.'

'Was it? That's strange. There was an engagement party in the village. The Prossers were there. So was I. After I'd spoken to you. They told me that you hadn't mentioned anything...'

'It wasn't a *lie*. They'd made a general sort of offer when I pitched the tent. I was on my way to the house to take them up on it.'

'But they'd already left. How convenient. What did you do then, Eleanor? Book yourself into a hotel? Go and wait in the pub, out of the storm?' It was obvious he didn't believe her. His voice was thick with sarcasm.

'No. I sat in my car, which I parked in a safe place. But if I hadn't caught up with them later I would have come back here and asked you for shelter for the night.' He wouldn't believe *that*, either. But at least she had the satisfaction of spelling out the truth. He could think what he liked.

'I'm supposed to believe that, am I?'

'Yes.'

'If I weren't so sure you were set on getting yourself killed I might be tempted to take you more seriously.'

'Getting myself killed! Oh, lord, we're not back to that unfortunate episode, are we? Look, I admit I nearly drowned. But I was petrified when I found out how close I'd come—I'd never swum in the sea before—I really didn't understand! I thought I'd got that across to you.'

'Oh, I did believe you. But that was yesterday. Now I know what a reckless little fool you really are I'm quite prepared to revert to my earlier opinion.'

'Me? Reckless? I'm no such thing!' Her grey eyes were wide with disbelief. Eleanor had been accused of many things in her life, but recklessness had never been one of them. She was aghast at the very idea.

'Eleanor, you have been in this village for precisely five days.' He spoke woodenly, as if he had suddenly been overcome by a vast weariness. 'In that time you have swum out into the Irish Sea, ridden a very big, very spirited horse who is much too strong for you, bareback and at full gallop, and sat for hours in a tent in a gale waiting to be crushed by a tree. Fortunately you lost patience. It *was* a bit of a long shot, after all.

'But I wish I'd realised you had already planted yourself on the edge of a cliff at midnight in the middle of a storm, waiting to be blown over the edge, before I lifted that damned tree off your tent. It was a bloody hard way of rescuing the mangled remains of your rucksack. It's just a shame Trenawr doesn't possess a bus service any longer. For your next trick you could have tried throwing yourself under the wheels.'

'Don't be absurd!' Her voice trembled with shock. 'I'm not trying to get myself killed! What an appalling thing to say!'

'What are you planning to do with the rest of your holiday, Eleanor? A little sunbathing in the path of a combine harvester? Barebacked parachuting? Or if this weather keeps up you could try windsurfing over to Dublin on a shopping spree.'

'Stop it! Stop it!' she cried, enraged beyond reason. 'I'm not like that. You've got me wrong!'

'Oh, no, I haven't,' he insisted viciously. 'You've got some kind of a death-wish driving you, little girl— whether you recognise it or not. Being bored to death by that piece of stuffed pork you called a fiancé was too slow a demise. But you haven't changed tracks, Eleanor. You're just accelerating the pace.'

'This is crazy! I'm *not* reckless, and I certainly don't have some kind of macabre death-wish driving me. Dear lord... If I were so very foolhardy, surely I wouldn't have refused to go to bed with you?'

'You mean you would have *made love* with me?' He spat the words out scornfully. Then he drew himself up to his full height, planted his hands on his hips and looked down on her. 'That decision only confirms my belief that your ambition in life is to completely self-destruct. It wouldn't have been the least bit foolhardy for you to have come into my bed, Eleanor. It would have been the most sublimely life-affirming thing you could have done. It would have been heartening... liberating... beautiful...'

It was there again. Despite everything he'd said, that sense of freedom, light and airy, had grabbed hold of her heart and was lifting it. He had accused her of un- believably awful things. He thought she was a fool. And, though he was wrong about the death-wish, he was very, very right about what it would have been like to make love with him. She just had to get him to understand...

'Listen to me, Gil. Please listen.'

'Go to bed,' he ordered coldly, with a decided air of finality. 'And try sleeping with your head on top of the pillow. It's safer.'

'No! You've accused me of terrible things, but they just aren't true. I didn't ride the gelding! And I was in the car—I really would have come here—you saw Mrs Prosser's letter, surely? And on the cliff—I knew what I was doing. I was perfectly safe...'

'Be quiet!' he roared. 'I know how your mind works. Find excuses. Deny the truth. I've seen you in operation, Eleanor. And I know how you responded to me out there in the storm, in the stable. I know how you felt when I kissed you! But the sort of risks which interest you don't have anything to do with pleasure, do they? Well, from now on don't expect me to kiss you again— or to try to save you from any more of your death-wish ventures.'

'You must hear me out! Don't I get a chance to defend myself?'

'No. If you stand here talking any longer in those wet clothes you'll get pneumonia. Or perhaps that's the general idea?'

'Gil, please...'

'No!' He roared out the word, turning his back on her and heading for the door.

'Gil...'

'Don't you know when you're beaten?'

Yes. Eleanor knew. He wasn't going to listen. Damn it, she really oughtn't care. She knew the truth, and that ought to be enough. Her pride reasserted itself.

'Yes. I know you won't listen to what I have to say,' she said stiffly. 'But there was something else——'

'Keep it brief.'

'It's just that I have no intention of sleeping in your bed again. If you could loan me a blanket——'

'What a good idea! The thatched stables in an electrical storm! Now that really would be a novelty——'

'Shut up!' She was almost screaming.

He looked at her coldly. 'You can have the room at the end. The bed is made up and it has its own bathroom.' His frozen gaze took in her drenched form. 'There are even clothes there you can borrow,' he added. 'You should survive the night.'

He went ahead of her out of the room. She watched his back disappear through the door, and held herself taut for a moment, before exhaling heavily. She didn't want to follow those muscular shoulders upstairs. She didn't want to get close to the man again tonight. She felt threatened by the power he had over her. But as she watched him go, a confident spring in his step, she knew that not being close to him again, ever, was going to be quite unbearable. It came into her mind with an outstanding clarity that she didn't just desire him. She loved him. And it had nothing at all to do with his having saved her life.

She must be going crazy. She was tired and cold and wet. She wanted a warm bath and a comfortable bed. She would feel differently in the morning. She hated him.

The room offered both. But it wasn't until she had closed the bedroom door that she understood that now, knowing that she loved Gil, this room was capable of making her burn with a raging jealousy. She picked up cushions and pillows from the bed and flung them with all her might across the room. At last there was just one pillow left. She considered it for a moment. If she slept completely flat, without any pillows, she might get more blood to her brain during the night. Her sanity would be restored. She would wake up and find her emotions back to normal. She picked up the last pillow and prepared to hurl it with all her might. What was it he had said about it being safer to sleep with her head on top of the pillow...? Oh, damn him. She flung the pillow back on to the bed. You just didn't win with someone like him.

While she ran the bath she went to look out something suitable to wear for the night. She found the drawer containing the embarrassingly skimpy underwear, and drew from it with the tips of her fingers a filmy black nightgown. Shocked by its translucence, she took the matching peignoir, too, in a feeble attempt to preserve a little more of her modesty than the nightgown alone would allow, and took them bitterly with her into the small ivory-coloured bathroom. She wished now that she had slept in his bed, after all, snug between the starched sheets. Even more did she wish she had gone with him when he had pleaded with her, and had made love and slept naked, safe in his arms.

CHAPTER SEVEN

'GOOD lord. What are you wearing?'

Eleanor scowled. 'I found it in the wardrobe. It was the only thing which seemed remotely suitable.' It was a tracksuit. But it was silver and flamingo-pink, and made from a material resembling parachute silk. It shimmered and flapped as she walked. On her feet she wore her damp, muddy climbing boots. Luckily he couldn't see the translucent coral pop-socks which she wore beneath them, or the skimpy lace underwear.

She avoided looking at him. It had been a long night. She had lain awake, listening to the storm blowing itself out and thinking.

'You look quite extraordinary in that outfit! It suits Sylvia, but it makes you look like——'

So it *was* Sylvia's room... 'A clown. I know.' She sighed heavily. 'Obviously this Sylvia and I have very different taste in clothes.'

'Obviously.'

'Who is she?' Her voice, she noted, had sounded quite normal. As if little needles weren't stabbing at her heart at the mere mention of the woman.

'Sylvia? She's my—— Oh, it's too complicated to explain. Let's just say that she likes to think she's my partner. She's not, as it happens, but I have to admit I've considered the idea. She's got a lot going for her, has dear Sylvia, but I'm keeping her dangling for a while. To see how she reacts. I doubt she'll stick around for much longer. She's an extraordinary woman, but she doesn't like to be kept waiting. My parents are very keen on the idea, though. My father thinks I owe it to her to make it legal, and he may be right. But I'm afraid I don't take advice on matters like that from anyone... Least of all from dear Papa. His morality and judgement in these matters is somewhat behind the times.'

Like mine, thought Eleanor nastily, before she registered that she was, in fact, glad that Gil didn't think a sexual relationship with Sylvia was reason enough for marrying the woman. 'Does she live here with you?' she asked next.

'Good gracious, no.'

'But all the clothes and stuff?'

He shrugged. 'We entertain here at times.'

'Where does she live?'

'Milford Haven.'

'Not far...'

'Far enough. Why are you so curious about Sylvia?'

'I'm not.'

'Well, you've asked enough questions about her.'

'Have I? I'm just trying to make conversation. To be polite.'

'Well, stop it. It gets on my nerves.'

There was a silence, during which Eleanor's slender, tracksuit-clad body shimmered sinuously across the kitchen, though her feet made the journey rather less elegantly. Jealousy was a terrible emotion. She'd never experienced it before. It made her want to empty the kettle over Gil's complacent head. How could he be so blasé about Sylvia when last night he'd practically begged her to make love with him? Admittedly he'd made it quite plain that the whole business would be no more than an unemotional, if ecstatic coupling as far as he was concerned. But, even so, he'd recognised that

Eleanor wasn't the type to take sex so lightly. You'd think he might have shown some embarrassment about Sylvia's role in his life, if only for the sake of Eleanor's feelings.

She looked at his hair, which was all that was visible of his head behind the newspaper. Walnut and chestnut and hazelnut shells, thick and tousled. She wanted to run her fingers through it, and bury her face in it and smell it. She looked down at the kettle, and felt her fingers twitch as they gripped the handle. For once in her life she felt extremely reckless. But she didn't hurl it at the newspaper mask. Instead she switched it on, and spooned some instant-coffee granules into a mug.

'Did you sleep well?' The question was muttered from deep behind the paper.

'Now who's making polite conversation?'

'Impolite, as it happens. I was about to continue by pointing out that it's ten o'clock. Oughtn't you have gone and fetched some more water at six?'

'Yes.' She had been horrified to discover that she'd slept so late and missed the early collection. But she wasn't going to let him glimpse her dismay. Somewhere around four a.m. her resolve had hardened. No matter what nasty tricks her emotions were playing on her, she was not going to allow herself to be swayed one jot by the arrogant Gilchrist Rhys. He was neither going to bewitch her nor hurt her. She was her own woman. As soon as she got back to London she was going to give Edward his ring back, and find herself a flat. From now on she lived life her own way.

'Ah. Good. It means I can give you another lesson in gratitude. I went on your behalf... The water's on the dresser.'

Whose way? Eleanor groaned inwardly then glanced across at the samples and gave Gil a sickly smile. 'Thank you,' she muttered insincerely. For once she would rather spoil the research than be in Gil's debt yet again.

And then she sighed dispiritedly and slumped into one of the kitchen chairs. They were exactly back where they had started, four days earlier. She was grudgingly thanking him for having made her collection, and he, presumably, was about to start haranguing her for her ingratitude in not thanking him for saving her life. The only difference being that last time he had been right—her life had been in danger. But this time she most certainly had been quite safe.

Ironically, somewhere around three in the morning, the rain beating against the windowpanes, the wind moaning outside, she had remembered seeing him lift that tree. She hadn't known it was him at the time, of course, but the memory had shaken her with its potency. Lifting a tree like that, with his bare hands, had been quite a feat. He was powerfully built and undoubtedly extremely strong. But when she had seen the dark shadow, bent and straining in the distance, she had imagined that it must be some work-hardened farm-labourer or quarryman. A man well used to extreme physical effort. A man of extraordinary power and strength.

Now as she looked across at Gil, hidden behind the business section of a Sunday newspaper, his shirt-sleeves folded back, his sinewy forearms revealed, she acknowledged with a crushing clarity that he was that man. She was every bit as moved by the sight as she had been by the memory. He had lifted a tree to save her life. Then he had gone to the cliff-edge in a howling gale on the same errand. It was hard not to feel something—even if gratitude wasn't exactly the name for the emotion which thumped within her as she surveyed his naked arms and hands. Edward wouldn't have done either. He'd have dialled 999 and let somebody else do it for him. Of that she could be absolutely sure.

'Gil...' she said openly. 'I really must thank you for your efforts last night. Even though I was quite safe, I do appreciate that you sincerely believed I needed your help. What you did was very heroic. Please don't think that I underestimate your concern.'

He lowered the paper and gave her a long, unintelligible look. It wasn't a very nice look. Then he upped the paper again and resumed reading.

She finished making her coffee, and started to sip at it. Well, she'd done her best. She'd thanked him as sincerely as she was able. She was damned if she was going to let herself be made to feel guilty. There would be no more guilt in her life. She would do what seemed right to her, regardless of what other people appeared to expect.

'I'll go back to the Prossers' soon. The weather's calmed down quite considerably.'

He must have finished whatever paragraph he was reading before he deigned to reply. At any rate, it was a little while before the paper came down again and he said coldly, 'Your tent is wrecked. Or hadn't you realised?'

'I shall get another.'

'It's Sunday. I don't even know if there's anywhere you can buy tents in Cardigan or Lampeter or those other vast, urban metropolises of West Wales. But if there is they won't be open on a Sunday.'

'I'll get one tomorrow. I can sleep at the Prossers' tonight.'

'No, you can't. They've got a load of petrified cara-vanners occupying every spare inch of space in their house.'

'How do you know?'

Gil flicked at the newspaper he was holding. 'I went to buy this earlier on. Gwen Jenkins told me. Apparently Enid Prosser had to buy three packets of breakfast cereal at seven this morning to feed them all. *Three* packets, mark you. It speaks for itself, doesn't it?'

'Then I'll find a hotel. There's bound to be some-where within easy driving distance, so that I can keep up the collections.'

Gil kept his paper in front of his face, but an arm emerged and gestured towards the dresser. 'The Yellow Pages is in the bottom cupboard. There are several hotels. But nowhere near as many as there are caravan and camping sites. I wouldn't be at all surprised to hear that all the local hoteliers have been out this morning buying in stocks of breakfast cereal, too. Few holidaymakers will have been intrepid enough to brave out a storm like that one last night. You probably don't realise how un-usual your own brand of recklessness is...'

Count to ten. Breathe deeply. You are your own person living your own life. His opinion doesn't matter.

'Thank you...' she murmured sweetly, and fetched the telephone book.

There was a long silence during which she perused the directory while he did the same to the business pages.

Then Gil said, 'Your parents rang.'

'My parents? But how did they know where I was staying?'

'They had the bright idea of ringing the local post office. Gwen Jenkins gave them my number.'

'Oh. What did you tell them?'

'I told them you were in the bath. I'd heard the water running.'

'Oh.' She wondered what her parents had made of the information that she was having a bath in the home of a strange man. Eleanor inadvertently coloured at the thought. Her automatic nervous system had not yet cottoned on to the fact that she was a new woman this morning—a woman who didn't care one bit what others might think of her. 'What did they say?' she asked weakly.

'They said could I please check that you didn't have the water too hot.'

'They didn't!' But she knew they had. They must have. No one could have made up something like that. Her mother always warned her . . . every single time she took a bath. She mostly had showers at home for just that reason.

'They—or rather, your mother—most certainly did. She asked me particularly to make quite sure . . .'

'She couldn't seriously have wanted you to come and put your hand in the water?'

'She thought I had a wife who could accomplish the mission for me. Gwen Jenkins, careful of your maidenly virtue, had seen fit to tell them that my phone number belonged to Gwyn and Enid Prosser. I got Gwen's cautionary phone call just moments before your mother rang. Gwen, apparently, has decided from her brief meeting with Edward that he isn't the man for you. She's been delighted to see the two of us spending so much time together, and didn't want your parents queering things at this early stage.'

Eleanor winced visibly. So now Gwen Jenkins was running her life too! This was awful. 'She needn't have worried,' she muttered sourly.

'That's exactly what I told her, Eleanor. You can be sure of that. Your maidenly virtue will be quite safe in my hands from now on.'

'Good.' Disappointment hung around the defiant word like a fog.

'I would have been surprised at your mother's request,' continued Gil caustically, 'but after last night's events I can quite understand why she's concerned that you might take it into your head to leap into a bathtub of scalding water...'

'Of course I wouldn't do that! *Nobody* could be that stupid... It's just that my mother once heard about a girl who fainted and——'

'Spare me the details.'

'Gladly,' muttered Eleanor with a sigh, inwardly lecturing herself for having responded to the comment about the scalding water so naïvely. Never mind. She would learn. She wasn't going to allow herself to become anyone's dupe ever again.

'What does she do when your father switches on a light? Notifies the fire brigade, I suppose?'

'She doesn't worry about my father,' murmured Eleanor with a frown. 'Only me.' It was true. Neither of her parents was particularly over-protective of the other. She'd not realised that before... It was odd, because, no matter what Gil thought, she had never been foolhardy. Her parents might think she was too strong-willed for her own good... too vehement... too different from them... But she knew that they trusted her, as they did each other. So why were they so fearful for her?

She began to dial a number of hotels in the locality. But, as Gil had predicted, all were bulging at the seams.

'You'll have to stay here,' growled Gil from behind his newspaper, after about the ninth abortive call.

'I'd die rather,' snapped Eleanor.

'Exactly,' came the disembodied voice, in a blood-curdlingly dismissive tone.

'I shall sleep in my car. The storm has died down now,' she returned furiously.

'Shall I help you find a nice parking spot on the cliff-top? The view will be magnificent. And I don't suppose you've had your hand-brake checked recently, have you? That should enhance the thrill enormously.'

'The car was serviced only a fortnight ago by a reputable—— ' She stopped herself. She was doing it again—taking his taunting seriously.

'I'm going for a walk,' she announced, reaching for her orange waterproof, which was hanging on the back of the kitchen door. Slipping it on, she found last night's sample still in the pocket. She removed the bottle and unknotted the long piece of twine which had been used for dangling it over the cliff-edge the previous day, and placed it with the others on the dresser.

'I was quite safe,' she found herself hissing as she let herself out of the door. Now why had she said that? She mustn't allow herself to care what he thought. She would go along the cliff and retrieve her harness and ropes. Now that she had made all her decisions she would be needing them. She could join that rock-climbing group again. She should never have let Edward make her resign. And go orienteering and fell-walking at weekends, too, as she'd used to. She would begin to enjoy life in her own way again, instead of lurking in that hinterland of other people's desires.

She hadn't got far before Jip joined her, bounding along, wagging his tail, his pink tongue lolling out of his grinning mouth. She reached out her hand and ruffled his back. Perhaps she'd get a dog once she'd found a flat. It would be good company. Her parents had never allowed her to have one in case it turned nasty and attacked her... She'd have to get a small one, though. It wouldn't be fair to get a big dog and keep it in London. It wasn't as if she needed a guard dog or anything. A small one would do. And if she found a research post her working hours might be more flexible than they were in the careers office, and she could manage to take it for plenty of long walks...

Out on the cliff-top, with just the dog and the breeze for company, she began to feel mournful. It was no good. When she looked at Gil she was filled with an almost worshipful feeling. She did love him. And it was going to make this new life of hers so much harder to tackle, endlessly having to quell that aching need...

Matters weren't helped when she heard a branch crack in the distance and turned to see him striding along behind. Obviously he really believed she wasn't fit to take a walk on her own. She felt a pang of self-disgust. How could she feel so much for a man who had such an appallingly low opinion of her? Was she so much lacking in self-respect?

Jip noticed Gil's presence, too. He wagged his tail furiously then gambolled off to his master's side. Having arrived there, he apparently decided that he missed Eleanor, and rather flatteringly charged back to join her. He looked up, panting and wheezing from the effort, then his eyes misted with indecision, and he hovered uncertainly for a moment before looping back towards Gil. Eleanor wanted to laugh. What a fool dear old Jip could be. She couldn't resist sneaking a look over her shoulder.

He was running flat out. At his age he really ought to take life a bit more easily, she reflected laughingly.

Again he joined Gil only to spy Eleanor in the distance, and again he hovered before making the return journey. This time, though, he was distracted halfway. A rabbit bolted out of the hedgerow across his path. Half wild with ecstasy, he increased his pace to follow the scudding tail. But Jip was an old dog. And at that point a very tired dog. The rabbit veered away from the cliff-edge with ease. But not poor Jip.

Eleanor reached the point where he had disappeared moments before Gil did. She flung herself flat on the grass and dragged herself the last six feet on her elbows. The cliff was quite sound at this point, but you could never be too careful. Gil came close beside her, still on foot.

'Get back,' she found herself urging nervously. 'And lie down. It's safer.'

He frowned at her briefly before dropping to his stomach alongside her. 'What the hell——?' he began.

'Listen!' she interrupted him. 'I can hear Jip howling.'

Gil edged forward to peer over the cliff.

'Stop!' she hissed anxiously, but he paid no attention. 'Gil...' she pleaded more gently. 'Come back from the edge. I'll go and get my rope and harness. We can assess the situation properly then...'

But Gil had already reached the edge and peered over. 'He's on a ledge,' he said heavily. 'About twenty feet down. He's standing up. He looks OK, but frightened to death.'

'Get back,' she moaned, and this time Gil inched backwards.

Clear of the edge, they found themselves staring into each other's eyes. 'Go and ring the coastguards,' Gil said harshly. 'I'm staying here.'

Eleanor gasped. She had not yet got over the shock of seeing him standing so close to the edge of the cliff. 'Gil . . . please . . . let me be the one to stay. I've had quite a lot of training in this sort of thing. I'll be quite safe.'

His dark brows almost met in the middle. His eyes glinted hard brown and murky green beneath them. 'Go and ring the coastguards. Quickly.' It was a command this time.

With a relieved awareness that he was quite capable of handling the situation, she shuffled further back before scrambling to her feet and fleeing without a backward glance towards the nearest house. Luckily it was the Prossers'. They would let her use the phone without wasting time on foolish questions.

When she returned she had her equipment with her, and a broken shot-gun over one arm.

Gil was still lying prone on the grass, listening to the pitiful howling of the dog.

She lay down her burden and dropped alongside him.

'Gil . . .' she said miserably. 'The coastguards can't raise anyone to help. Apparently there's a trawler lying about fifteen miles off shore, badly damaged by last night's storm. All the services are tied up in getting the crew safely off. But I've brought everything we need to go down for him. I managed to get a good view of the situation back along the path a bit. The rock structure is very sound here—there's no risk of landslip, and there's a sturdy oak we can use for anchorage in the field back there. Gwyn Prosser will be along to help as soon as he can, but he's got a cow in labour at the moment, and I don't think we ought to wait . . .'

He looked at her blankly for a moment, as if he could scarcely bring himself to register what she was saying. 'You mean to tell me that you're planning a one-woman rescue mission?' he said scornfully. 'Now I've heard everything.'

'No,' she continued as calmly as she could managed. 'Not a one-woman mission, Gil. It will be a two-person mission. I can't do it without your help. I'll go over and abseil down. I've brought a strong zip-top bag from the Prossers' to put Jip in. I have all the proper equipment. You'll be in charge of the ropes up here. I can tell you exactly what to do. It will be perfectly safe. I wouldn't have suggested it otherwise.'

He shook his head dismissively. 'Absolutely not. I'll go and ring our engineering workshops. We have our own helicopters and——'

'No, Gil,' she sighed despairingly, trying to shut off Jip's pitiful cries from her mind. 'You and your employees are marine engineers—not air-sea rescue personnel. It would be incredibly dangerous. Anyway, it would take far too long.' She nodded at the shot-gun lying on her pack of equipment. 'Gwyn gave me that. He said you'd know how to use it. If we can't do this together, surely it would be far kinder to use it now and put poor Jip out of his undoubted misery.'

Gil's gaze positively burned with intensity. She couldn't even begin to imagine what was going through his mind as she looked deep and hard into her eyes. At long last he said, 'I'll go over the edge. Not you. You can tell me what to do.'

Briefly Eleanor closed her eyes. So much for her resolution not to justify herself in his eyes. Now she had no choice. It was a matter of life or death for Jip that she convince him of her trustworthiness. 'It won't work

that way, Gil. You see we don't know what the rock face
is like. I can tell you how to abseil down, certainly, but
if the rock is unclimbable I wouldn't have the strength
to haul you back up. But you could pull me up quite
easily. My life will be in your hands... It's the only way.
The only safe way. I'm experienced, Gil. Very experienced. You must believe that. For goodness' sake, you
saw me roped and harnessed last night—and I knew what
I was doing——'

'You were what?'

'Surely you knew? Good grief! I jolted backwards hard
enough when I reached the end of the rope.'

'I thought you'd pulled away on purpose... I thought
you were determined to go your own way——'

'No. It was the rope. The harness, as you are about
to discover, is soaking wet and muddy. It's been lying
in that field since last night.' She kept looking steadfastly into his eyes. He continued to stare back, his eyes
clouded. But at least he didn't reach for the gun.

Eleanor turned away slowly and began to open her
pack. She extracted the coils of rope and several other
items, and made for the tree. He didn't stop her. In fact
he came to watch as she deftly secured the ropes, testing
every item methodically and thoroughly. All the while
Jip's howls could be heard, carried faintly on the breeze.
She still didn't know whether he would allow her to go
down or not, but, taking a deep breath, she began to
explain exactly what would happen, step by step, as she
completed her preparations. Then she clambered into the
harness and secured it.

'No!' he exclaimed harshly. 'I'll go.'

Eleanor looked into his eyes. 'All right,' she sighed.
'If you get stuck I can lock the ropes so you won't fall.
But you'll have to hang there until the coastguards can

get something organised. It might be a long time from what they said on the phone . . .'

His eyes flickered away from her to the cliff-edge, from where Jip's desperate whining could be heard.

'If that were to happen, can you use the shot-gun?' he asked stiffly.

She shook her head. He rubbed at his chin, then turned back to her. 'I'll take charge of the ropes,' he said decisively.

Briefly she explained what had to be done, then set off for the cliff-edge. She felt an astonishing confidence as she began her descent, knowing that her life was safe in his strong brown hands.

She had done this many times, and she could hardly claim to be nervous. Yet every time she went over the edge she would feel that old surge of adrenalin, that thrill of fear, which made the venture so rewarding as a sporting exercise. But this time it was no sport. She was doing it for real. Jip's life depended on her, and her own on Gil. She pushed the thoughts from her mind, calling out to Gil as she disappeared from his sight, reassuring him that Jip was still safe.

It took only a couple of minutes before she was securely beside Jip on the ledge. It was reasonably broad and felt sound. She knelt beside him while he whimpered, and began cajoling him into the bag. Jip was shaking, frightened to death. He liked Eleanor, but he didn't know her well enough to trust her implicitly.

At last she was forced to call out to Gil, 'He won't get into the bag for me. It's no good. I'm only frightening him more, and I'm afraid that if I do anything to startle him he'll back off and go over the edge. I just don't know enough about dogs and how they react to risk it. I'm coming back up.'

The ascent was considerably slower, though the cliff-face proved relatively easy to climb. When her face finally appeared over the top she found Gil staring transfixed at her, his features set and hard beneath the tan. Once she was kneeling safely on the grass Gil let go his hold of the ropes and reached for the gun. She scrambled across to him and laid a hand on his arm.

'No, Gil. Not yet. You go down. You'll be able to persuade him into the bag. He trusts you. I'll take charge of the ropes. You'll manage the climb without any problems.'

There was a silence while he looked into her face as if searching for something he had no expectation of finding. Then he said, unexpectedly and curtly, 'Take off the harness.' He was prepared to put his own life into her hands.

Eleanor had guided any number of youngsters over the edge. For several years she had worked as a youth leader in her spare time and had often helped the outward-bound instructor on ventures of this sort. She had never been afraid for them as she had watched their frightened white faces disappear, knowing that what they were doing was considerably safer than it looked. But watching Gil disappear from sight was something quite different. Only the knowledge that she must not falter kept her voice steady as she kept up a reassuring flow of chatter. Inside her blood thundered in her veins and roared in her ears. She loved Gil, and yet she had just encouraged him to go over the edge of a cliff, hundreds of feet above a boiling ferment of sharp rocks and crashing waves. Her mouth was parched with fear. She almost cried aloud with relief when she felt the rope go slack and heard Gil shout, 'It's OK...'

The minutes of waiting while he persuaded the reluctant dog into the bag seemed an eternity. And then her mind locked back on to the job in hand while he began his ascent.

He was a strong, fearless athlete, and made the return trip more speedily than she had. As he heaved himself on to the grass she began to shake uncontrollably. He was safe. Thank God he was safe. She pressed her trembling fingers prayerfully against her eyes. It was left to Gil to haul the poor dog back beside them. By that time Eleanor's knees had buckled and she was kneeling on the grass, trying to steady her hands, her teeth chattering. He came close to her and put his arms around her. Jip lolloped towards them and jumped on them, wagging his tail, trying to lick their faces. Together they tumbled backwards on the cold, wet grass, Gil's arms still holding her tight, his fingers digging into her shoulder-blades. His face loomed above hers. She felt sure that he was going to kiss her.

Painfully she forced herself to tuck in her chin, ducking her head away from his, pressing her cheek to his chest. She couldn't pull away. She was too weak with relief, and anyway Jip was still jumping all over them. But she wouldn't let him kiss her. For just a moment she let herself savour the sensation of his smooth shirt against her face. It smelt cleanly of cold rainwater and ironing. Through it she heard his heart thud steadily, and sensed the warmth of his blood beneath the hair-roughened skin. Oh, how she loved him. She closed her eyes. He trusted her now. He had put his own life in her hands. There could be no more proof needed than that. And yet it wasn't enough.

'Eleanor?' he murmured. 'Thank you. I was a fool——'

'No.' The word was torn from her, bloody and ragged. 'Don't say anything. Please.'

He had chosen from the outset to think badly of her. He had mocked her and teased her and used her. He had some rich bitch dangling on a string, hoping for a marriage which he had no intention of providing. Only a fool would succumb because he had finally accepted that she wasn't the complete idiot he had liked to imagine her to be. Still she breathed in the scent of him and yearned for it to be different.

'But I was wrong. I——'

'I don't want to hear. I just want you to let me go and get on with my own life. Please...' Her voice was stiff with the effort of controlling her desires. Let him be the one to go. Please. So that she didn't have to use any more of her precious will-power pulling away from him and standing up and turning her back. But he continued to hold her, his broad palms moving gently, soothingly against her back.

Would she have gone on resisting if Gwyn Prosser hadn't appeared just then, standing beside them, and laughing loudly? He picked up the shot-gun.

'I knew you wouldn't be needing that,' he smiled. 'Now if you'll excuse me I must be off. I'll look in on Gwen Jenkins on the way, though, and tell her that all's well. She'll be delighted.'

Eleanor freed herself from Gil's arms and got to her feet. He was watching her, propped on one elbow on the grass. She looked at her watch.

'I've missed the noon collection. But for once it couldn't be helped,' she said levelly, meeting his eye as boldly as she dared.

He didn't reply. He just went on looking at her. Looking and looking at her. And then she mustered her will-power and bundled her equipment together and set off.

CHAPTER EIGHT

ELEANOR had finished crying quite early that morning, for a change, and had patched up her face before lying on her stomach in her new tent, trying to concentrate on her book. She didn't look up when she heard horses' hoofs approaching. There was no point. It wouldn't be him. If he'd wanted to speak to her he knew perfectly well that she had a regular date with the sea every six hours, seven days a week. She'd made her final collection at six that morning. He hadn't come. After lunch she would pack up and begin the long drive home. She wouldn't see him again now—not that she wanted to, anyway. That animal part of her, awakened from its long sleep, wanted to see him, to be near him, of course. But the rest of her didn't.

He stuck his head in through the open flap of the tent.

'Hi!' he said, as if they were the best of friends. 'Budge up, I'm coming in.'

She had no choice. He was already blocking the entrance with his body. She scuttled as fast as she could to the far end of the tent, and sat there, her knees clasped beneath her chin, glowering at him.

'Good lord,' he murmured, looking at the space she had vacated. 'I didn't realise you thought you might have broken my heart.'

She let out a tight, angry sigh. 'You don't have a heart to break. Anyway, as usual I haven't the least idea what you're talking about.'

He sat comfortably beside her, filling most of the space with his long, loosely coiled frame. 'You left me so much room, Eleanor. Quite disproportionate to my size. I assumed you must be imagining that I've been on a binge of "comfort eating" since last we met, and must have gained masses of weight.'

His wry comment drew her eyes to his spare well-muscled torso, outlined beneath his faded, open-necked shirt. She had no sooner looked than she wished she hadn't. He was just as damned attractive as ever. It was infuriating. Here she was, on the threshold of taking hold of her life, and all she wanted to do was to look at *him*.

'That was a particularly unfunny joke,' she muttered sourly.

'I agree,' he said, offering her a gaze loaded with rueful charm. 'I'm afraid I've not been on form since you walked off. Where did you spend Sunday night, anyway?'

'Gwen Jenkins offered me a bed. *Without* insisting that I grovel with gratitude.' She let her lip curl with obvious distaste. Eleanor had had virtually no experience of being intentionally impolite. But she fancied she was catching on quickly. It was rather enjoyable, she found, feeling free to express her dislike of him so openly.

'Really?' he said lightly. Then he added, 'I've come to take you out.'

'Feel free to get *out* of this tent any time you like. But don't expect me to accompany you.'

'Is that an invitation? Then thank you. I'll stay.'

She groaned, pressing her hands to her face. 'Go away,' she growled. Then she puffed out her cheeks and let out a noisy sigh.

'I've brought Molly to see you.' His voice was soft, cajoling.

One corner of her mouth tightened, and she let her eyes roll slightly in an expression of dismissive scorn. 'Who on earth is Molly, and why should I want to meet her?'

'The little grey mare. And you look like Groucho Marx.'

She curled her upper lip and let her eyes roll even further back in her head.

He threw back his own head and laughed. 'Seriously! You look absurd, pulling all those dreadful faces.'

She returned her features to their more natural scowl. 'Why do you endlessly try to belittle me?'

'I'm not. I'm simply telling the truth. Look, Eleanor——' he gazed seriously into her eyes '—the thing is, if you really want to wither people with a glance you have to spend half your adolescence in your bedroom practising all these little facial gestures in the dressing-table mirror. Otherwise you just end up looking bizarre.'

She felt her face redden. 'You know this from experience, do you?' she said acidly.

He laughed again. 'As it happens, I'm a natural-born boor. I've never needed to practise. Come for a ride and I'll tell you all about my filthy moods.'

'I know everything I need to know about your filthy moods, thank you.'

'Except,' he said grasping her wrist and scrambling out of the tent, pulling her with him, 'that sometimes— but only sometimes, mind you, and only when I'm in a very, very good mood—I get around to apologising for my outbursts.'

She straightened up and looked hard into his eyes. 'You mean you've come to apologise unreservedly for

all the awful things you've accused me of? I don't believe it.'

'And nor should you. Of course I haven't,' he grinned
wickedly. 'Come on, get up on Molly.'

She glanced at the gentle animal, weakening slightly.
It would be so nice to go riding once more before she
returned to London. But not with Gil. 'No,' she said
heavily, and stooped to crawl back into her tent.

But he caught her by the waist and swung her up into
the air as if she were as light as a feather, and dumped
her flat on her stomach across Molly's saddle. Her feet
flailed for a moment until she found a stirrup and
managed to straddle the horse properly. She grimaced
at him, and then, remembering his wry comments, composed her features expressionlessly.

He mounted the gelding with a swift, easy grace, and
then leaned over, caught hold of Molly's reins and began
guiding them both out of the orchard.

'I said I didn't want to come!' she remonstrated.

'But you want me to apologise, don't you?'

'I couldn't care less. Anyway, you just told me that
you had no intention of apologising.'

'No, I didn't. I said I wasn't going to apologise for
everything. It doesn't mean I'm not going to apologise
for anything.'

'Riddle-me-ree...' she muttered sarcastically.

He flung her an amused glance. 'Molly's just about
the right size for you,' he commented, adding, 'You look
good on horseback.'

'I thought you didn't trust me near a horse.'

'That was before I realised you hadn't ridden Satan,
but only led him through to the fields and let him have
a run. Gwen Jenkins told me that Lily Matthews had
told her that Rhian Jones had said you only rode Molly.'

'Of course I only rode Molly. I'm not such a fool, as you ought to have known from the start.'

'As it happens, my misunderstanding over the horses is the one thing I'm prepared to apologise for. It was just that when I found that the only piece of tack which had appeared to have been disturbed was Satan's bridle I naturally assumed——'

'You needn't have believed the worst. It was the only thing I hadn't had time to clean and put back in place. I accept that you realise now that you'd got me badly wrong. But I don't accept that any of your vicious assumptions were justified in the first place. I don't trust a man with judgement as bad as yours.' And with that she stopped the plodding horse, dismounted and began to march away from him as fast as she could.

He turned Satan, nudged him into a canter, and swept by her, scooping her off the ground with one arm as he rode past. He hauled her unceremoniously across the horse's neck in front of him. Her hair hung down over her face on one side, and her legs kicked out on the other.

'Stop it!' he shouted. 'You'll upset Satan. You don't want him to bolt, do you?'

Since she was hanging upside-down across the horse, that was, needless to say, the last thing she wanted. She went limp, until Gil had manoeuvred the big horse alongside Molly. 'Now get back on,' he ordered. 'You're coming with me. There's something I want to show you.'

'No.'

'Yes. And be quick about it, or we'll be too late.'

'Nobody orders me about any more, Gil,' she said fiercely.

But he paid no attention, simply scooping her up once again and plonking her in the saddle. Then he caught hold of Molly's reins and began to move off at a fast trot. Molly fell into step beside Satan. Trotting, Eleanor realised, was an art which one never forgot. It was also an art which required a certain amount of concentration if one was not either to fall off or end up very saddle-sore. Particularly if one did not have control of the reins. She resigned herself to having to accompany him a little further.

Their destination was, as she had suspected, Gil's house. Once on solid ground again he grabbed hold of her wrist and pulled her swiftly through to the garden.

'Sit there and watch,' he muttered quietly, pushing her into one of the wrought-iron chairs and lowering himself into the seat beside her.

At first she couldn't make out what it was she was supposed to be looking at. She glanced across at Gil's profile. His eyes were fixed intently on the bough of a tree. She followed his gaze until, with a start of pleasure, she realised what it was that he had brought her to see. Three or four young blue-tits, downy-fresh from the nest, were sitting precariously on the branch. The parent birds were fussing around a hole in the trunk, fifteen or sixteen inches higher.

'Oh! I see what you mean!' murmured Eleanor softly, her eyes transfixed. Suddenly she didn't feel quite so bad about his having forced her to accompany him. She wouldn't have wanted to miss seeing this for the world.

'Watch the parent birds,' said Gil. 'They're tempting them out.'

'So they are. Do all birds do that?'

'No. Some wait until the fledgelings pack their own little bags and flounce out in a tantrum.'

'Good gracious! That's six I've counted out already... No... seven...'

'That's nothing. Blue-tits can lay anything up to twelve eggs in a clutch.'

'Really? They're such tiny little birds. You wouldn't think they'd have the strength, would you? Oh, look at that one trying to fly. He can't get the hang of it at all. They're such babies still, aren't they?'

Gil didn't respond directly. He had stopped watching the birds, and had started watching her. She shifted uncomfortably in her chair, conscious of his scrutiny.

'Come on inside and have some lunch,' he murmured.

Another of his fry-ups, no doubt. Well, she'd pass up the offer today. She wanted to forget all about him as soon as possible... Eating his food was no way to start.

'Sorry. Not today. I'll just wait to see that poor little one safely back into the nest and then I'll go.'

'You'll have a long wait. It won't be going back into the nest, and neither will any of the others.'

'But that one on the grass—and look, there's another couple over there—they aren't ready to look after themselves. They can't even fly properly yet. They'll die if they're just left there!'

'Eleanor, please don't use that hectoring tone with me. I have a lot of influence in certain spheres. But I cannot interfere with the private lives of these blue-tits. I don't speak the language for a start. Now can we please go inside and eat our lunch, and give the cat a bit of privacy to eat his?'

'That's a terrible thing to say!'

'No, it's not. Eleanor, do you know why the parent birds are so anxious to get rid of their huge brood so quickly?'

'No.'

'They're hoping to hatch another dozen eggs before summer's out. They're running out of time. And so are we. Come on.'

'But we can't just leave them . . .'

'We can. A lot of blue-tit chicks don't survive. But a hell of a lot do. They're one of the most numerous birds in Britain. Don't worry about them. It's just nature's way.'

'But if the cat——'

'That particular fledgeling might not provide lunch for the cat. If we clear off a much rarer species of bird— a sparrowhawk or an owl for instance—might chance by and pick it off, and take it back to its own nest to feed to its own young. You surely don't want to see a poor, fluffy little round-eyed owlet starve to death, do you? Eleanor! I never imagined you could be so cruel!'

'It's those parent birds who are cruel, not me! It may be nature's way, but——'

'Nature, as you ought to know, is "red in tooth and claw". But the birds aren't cruel. They're simply following their instincts. As you yourself should. Aren't you hungry? And afterwards, wouldn't you like to make love with me? You see, Eleanor—nature has its sweeter side too. Now if you just let your instincts surface——'

'Oh, so we're back on that boring old subject, are we? Me and my instincts? You and your promiscuous sex-drive, more like!'

He took her arm and started to lead her towards the house. 'Actually,' he smiled, 'the parent birds aren't following their own instincts at all. It only seems that way. In fact they're responding instinctively to the needs of the young.'

'You mean to tell me those babies want to be chucked out of the nest to be eaten by a cat? Come off it. You were the one who pointed out the parent birds calling them out of the nest.'

'Yes. But last year they behaved quite differently, you know. They raised just one chick—very successfully, as it happens. It was bigger and stronger and more fearless than they were. They didn't push that one of the nest. In fact they followed the chick around for weeks after it had flown, feeding it extra titbits.'

'Why?'

'Because that's what the chick demanded from them. It was a cuckoo. Which brings us rather nicely back to the subject of you, don't you think?'

'What do you mean? That I'm a cuckoo in my parents' nest? Charming!'

They were in the dining-room now. Eleanor looked in astonishment at the table. It was immaculately laid for two. Crystal goblets sparkled amid the heavy, gleaming silverware. A huge silver bowl of roses graced the centre of the table.

He pulled out a chair to seat her. Eleanor stood defiantly and glared at him. 'You're so sure of yourself, aren't you? So sure of getting your own way. You treat me appallingly—use me to amuse yourself, then totally ignore me for days on end. And when you get bored you decide to look me up to see if you can provide yourself with a few more hours of sport at my expense. What's more, when I refuse to play along you actually throw me on to a horse like some character in a third-rate Wild-West movie, as if my wishes didn't matter at all. Well, tough, because I'm not——' She stopped abruptly.

A throat had been cleared somewhere behind her left shoulder.

Eleanor glanced in the direction of the noise. A plump woman of around forty was standing in the doorway holding a large tureen of soup in her hands, and smiling uncertainly.

Could politeness be instinctive? Eleanor concluded that it must be. It was the only explanation she could think of for the meek way in which she suddenly slipped into her seat, smiling reassuringly at the woman. It just suddenly seemed impossible to storm out while the woman hovered expectantly, the tureen in her hands.

Gil nodded his acknowledgement to the woman, and sat himself opposite. 'Eleanor,' he said courteously, 'I'd like you to meet Sîan Williams, my housekeeper and the wife of my farm manager.'

'Hello,' smiled Eleanor politely, relieved to have been introduced. She had never been in a house with servants, and had already demonstrated quite effectively that she was not able to treat them as if they didn't exist. Which was the way, she gathered from novels she read, they ought to be treated. She was glad that Gil didn't seem to take that attitude either.

Sîan Williams served the soup—a delicate watercress, sprinkled with freshly grated nutmeg—and then left.

'Perhaps I should explain that I've been away on business since early Monday morning. Or I would have looked you up earlier to entice you into my arms. However, a little crisis in one of the Gulf ports required my immediate presence. Nothing less would have dragged me away from Trenawr at such an auspicious time.' He offered her a smile of unremitting charm.

She was tempted to return it with one of her withering looks, but, remembering his earlier comments, decided otherwise.

'But I'm being inconsiderate,' he continued silkily. 'You were in the middle of saying something when Sîan appeared?'

The smile he produced while pouring out the chilled white wine was positively smug. He thought he had only to smirk sweetly and she would come running. Oh, the arrogance of the man!

'I was saying that I had no intention of eating with you. Did Mrs Williams cook this?'

'Yes.'

'Then as a courtesy to her I shall change my mind. But I wish to stress that every morsel that passes my lips does so on her account, and not yours. I know no ill of her and if she has gone to all the trouble of cooking me a meal I shall do nothing intentionally to offend her.'

Gil smiled over his soup spoon. He said not a word.

Still in the grip of her instinctive politeness, Eleanor found herself speaking again. 'I think you've got a nerve, comparing me to a cuckoo. You know three insignificant things about my family. That's all. And yet you've labelled me a cuckoo in the family nest.'

'Four things.'

'Three! I've had five days to reflect on our conversations and I know exactly how much I've told you about myself and my parents. One, you know that my mother makes dreadful porridge. Two, you know that they worry about the temperature of my bath water. And three, you know that they don't like me to swim in the sea.'

'Four,' continued Gil, clearly amused, 'I know that they like you to ring to say that you've got to work safely.'

She narrowed her grey eyes. 'OK. Four. It's not a lot.'

'It's enough.'

'So I'm a cuckoo because my mother makes horrible porridge?'

'I didn't say that you were a cuckoo, Eleanor. You said it yourself. How could I have said such a thing when it's so patently obvious that you're very much a human being, not a bird?' His eyes were raking over her seductively.

'Then what *do* you mean?' retorted Eleanor, wishing that she had decided to dress more circumspectly that morning. The brief sun-top and shorts were only encouraging him. 'That I want my parents to behave as they do? They've always driven me crazy with their fussing.'

'I don't think you want them to behave like that. No. But perhaps they don't have a choice.'

Eleanor frowned, bending her head over her soup plate. She didn't want to be having this conversation with Gil. It was pointless anyway. She'd applied her considerable intelligence to the problem of her parents times without number. And she always concluded simply that they loved her, she loved them, but they were incompatible. The only point at issue was how much she bent to their will, and that, so far, had varied according to the seasons of her life. As a toddler, apparently, she had yielded not at all. Lately she had yielded rather too much. In between it had varied . . . but the conflict had always been there.

Scallops arrived on a bed of crisp lettuce, interrupting her contemplations and forcing her to look up. Gil was watching her. She looked down again. All this time in his presence was having its predictable effect on her body. She squirmed uncomfortably in her seat.

At last Gil spoke. 'Last year's cuckoo finally took off for Africa. This year the parent birds are back to relying on their own instincts and doing what nature intended for them.'

'Is that an ornithology lesson or a comment on my life?'

'Work it out.'

'You mean that if I go to Africa my parents will have a dozen babies within a year? Wow!'

He laughed—that deep, rumbling laugh of his that carved the hooped lines into his cheeks, that set his eyes sparkling and his nostrils quivering.

'It's all too simplistic, Gil. Sorry. But, as you yourself said, we're not birds. Our lives are a little more complicated than that.'

'Why have you never left home, Eleanor? You can be fearless enough at times, after all.'

It was a valid question. But she simply shrugged. She no longer wanted to explain herself to him. It wouldn't make him think any the better of her. He would merely use the information to taunt her further.

'Why didn't you leave when you went to university?' he persisted. 'Surely it would have been a natural time for the parting of the ways.'

'I . . .' Eleanor sighed. Oh, well. She might as well explain. After all, they had to talk about something while they ate.

'I made the mistake of taking myself seriously, Gil,' she said drily. 'I knew exactly what aspects of geology interested me. The course I really wanted to do more than anything was at the University of London. I thought then that it mattered that I studied the right subjects. But because my college was within easy reach of my home I didn't get the full student grant. I couldn't afford a flat. And though I tried to work part-time to increase my income I found it interfered with my studies. At the time that seemed more important than anything.'

'So why didn't you go on and do your research? Why did you stop taking yourself seriously? Truthfully, Eleanor.'

'My father was taken into hospital with chest pains shortly after my finals. I felt... well, I felt that I ought to try harder to please my parents after that. I'd been worrying them to death for nearly twenty-two years. It seemed about time I stopped.'

'I'm sorry,' said Gil gently. 'And how's your father's heart now?'

'Fine.'

'Good. Did he have by-pass surgery or what?'

'Oh, no. Nothing like that. It turned out that he only had a touch of pleurisy. There never was anything wrong with his heart.'

Gil's groan was loud enough to be classed as a bellow. It stopped Sîan Williams in her tracks as she cleared away the plates. 'I take it back!' he roared. 'All that stuff about you being a cuckoo! I take it back. You're three of a kind, you and your parents! You're *all* bloody cuckoo!'

Eleanor sat looking at him, open-mouthed in astonishment.

'Good lord...' he moaned. 'You give up your entire future as a scientist just because you're afraid that your father might one day genuinely be ill! Don't you realise that across the world there are millions of people—often young and full of vitality—who go on striving to get the most out of life despite the most awful handicaps? Real handicaps. Real illnesses. I once knew a girl who sat her exams in hospital, knowing full well that she'd never find out whether or not she'd pass or fail... And yet you give up because of some imaginary fear...some five-minute panic over a stupid chest infection! Honestly,

Eleanor, I'm beginning to believe that you must actually like being unhappy. It's ingrained, isn't it?'

His eyes sheared her, razor-sharp with scorn, and bitterly cruel.

'Gil ... I ...' But the instinct to be polite suddenly fled to be replaced by a deep, scalding anger. Eleanor leant, red-faced, across the table, her grey eyes bright, her arms folded in front of her. Mrs Williams set down the dishes of baby vegetables and the salver of chicken breasts in a wine sauce, and hurried embarrassedly out of the room.

'Stop it!' she shouted. 'You don't understand anything about me! I didn't change my lifestyle to suit my parents just in case my father should ever really get ill. I did it because ... because my mother burst into tears in the hospital corridor and ... and ...' Oh, damn it. She was crying herself now. Great, hot, angry tears which spilled out of her eyes in a torrent. But she was practically choking with the need to get this brute of a man to listen to her. She had no time to worry about the tears ...

'And she was so frightened, and she said that although she loved me and she knew I loved her I didn't understand her the way my father did, and if he died she'd be so alone ... Well,' she sniffed loudly, 'I just thought it was about time I tried to make the effort to get closer to them so that they wouldn't feel ... I mean, it seemed awful that they'd cared so much for me, and when the time came I couldn't even be a proper comfort to them because I was so different.'

He was staring at her expressionlessly.

'Oh, what's the point?' she continued. 'You wouldn't understand. You'll only find some way of turning it all about and making me look a fool again.'

'Eleanor ...' he said in a low voice.

'Shut up. Don't say a word or I'll tip a plate of food over your head. I don't want your comments. One of the reasons I came to Trenawr was to sort my life out. Well, at least I'm certain of one thing now: I never want to see *you* again!' And with that she got to her feet and started to walk away.

'You haven't finished your meal,' came his voice, softly, from somewhere behind her.

Anger fountained up inside her again. She turned swiftly back to the table. 'Oh, no. So I haven't. Well, I should hate to offend Mrs Williams.' And, still standing, she furiously spooned portions of food on to her plate. Then she picked it up and turned back towards the door. 'I'll wash the plate and leave it with Mrs Jenkins. If there's a pudding, do apologise to Mrs Williams for me, but tell her that I was full, anyway, and that she's a wonderful cook...'

She had stormed through the hall and the sitting-room and was through the french doors and halfway across the garden when he caught up with her. He took the plate from her, but she didn't pause, just kept marching forwards, her face set in bitter lines, the tears rolling faster than ever.

The plate moved gracefully through the air, spinning like a frisbee, before it hit a tree and smashed loudly into a thousand pieces. Still she didn't stop. It was *his* Spode dinner service. Let him smash it all to smithereens if he wanted. She'd had enough.

She hadn't counted on his strength. She was through the pergola and in the hidden part of the garden, which had a gate opening into the woods, before he grabbed hold of her. And turned her. And kissed her.

It was wonderful. Despite the fact that she was struggling against the iron strength of his arms, despite the fact that she hated him, and had no intention of being manipulated by him, the sensation of his warm mouth covering hers, probing and prying against her closed lips, his fingers hard against her pliant flesh—despite all that—it was stupidly, infuriatingly wonderful and she hated him for it.

It was also brief. He pulled his mouth away from hers and said harshly, 'Stop fighting it. You know it's right...'

'No!' she cried. 'No! No! You can't make me—I won't be made to do anything—especially by you—not ever again...'

His hands went to her shoulders, cupping their silken nakedness, sweeping down her upper arms to her elbows, holding her firmly. Then one thumb flicked out and stroked at her nipple. She flinched at the sharp stab of pleasure which jumped inside her. Her nipples stood hard and proud beneath the clinging cotton jersey of her sun-top.

'Stop it...' she wailed breathlessly, aching to fold herself against him and open her mouth and her body to his.

'Eleanor...Eleanor...' His voice was soft, low, pleading now. 'Make love with me, Eleanor. Let yourself. You know you want to...' And his hand cupped her breast, and his lips pushed at the clinging fabric, tugging it downwards until the creamy orb spilled out into his hand. His mouth came down upon her nipple, arousing such tantalising sensations that she cried out aloud. But her hands were clenched, the nails biting into her palms.

'No... No...' she groaned, sinking to her knees to escape the drifts of desire which threatened to overwhelm her. When she dared look up he was standing, feet astride, the fabric of his jeans taut across his thighs, revealing the strength of his own arousal. His eyes were lowered to meet hers. And the expression on his face was one she had never seen there before. The face which was turned towards her was marked not with disdain, but with such sweet tenderness that longing swelled and broke inside her, like a wave.

But if she were to yield to him, where would he take her? His room? Or Sylvia's? She scrambled to her feet and began to run. This time he didn't follow.

CHAPTER NINE

THE leaves were colouring under autumn's spell when she next drove through that part of Wales. The sheep looked fatter, less scraggy, now that their shorn coats had regrown. The hedgerows which had been white with blossom were dark with blackberries and sloes. She couldn't help remembering, although she had taken great care to use a route which took her nowhere near Trenawr. Aberystwyth was thirty miles away. She was no more likely to bump into him there than she would be to bump into an inhabitant of Reading in Oxford. But her mouth was dry at the very idea that somehow their paths might cross.

It was ridiculous, she scolded herself, still to feel that way about him. He certainly wouldn't have wasted any of his time thinking about her. All that stuff about them having something special going for them hadn't amounted to much, when all was said and done. He'd let her walk away from him without so much as speaking her name. She must have been mistaken about the expression on his face.

Her puppy whined in the back of the car. It had been a long drive and he was bored.

'It's OK,' she said soothingly to him. 'It's not far now. I'll take you for a long walk after I've had my interview.'

The lady at the dog's home had assured her that he would end up quite small. But already he was huge, and he was only half grown. It was her own fault for buying a mongrel, but there was something about his rough

165

black coat and the foolish way he seemed to grin, his pink tongue lolling out the side of his mouth, that had made him seem irresistible.

She ran her tongue over her dry lips. At least all this nervous tension about Gil was keeping her mind off the interview. The job was exactly what she wanted—it could have been tailor-made for her. She wanted it more than she'd ever wanted anything in her whole life. But not more than she'd wanted *anyone*, clearly, or she wouldn't be feeling so uptight about what could only be the remotest of remote possibilities...

She grinned through the car window at the animal, who was by now frantic to get his promised exercise. She opened the car door and let him leap all over her, stooping to hug him briefly, before straightening up. Suddenly she froze. It was only footsteps, crunching across the gravel of the car park behind her. They could be anybody's. Only a madwoman would believe that a footfall could be as distinctive as a voice, a scent, a smile...

His hands dropped on to her shoulders, and deftly, gently turned her around.

'Congratulations...'

'Oh...' The word caught in her throat. His voice. His scent. His smile. She had been right. She took in a breath and let it out with a shuddering gasp, then bit on her lower lip to quell the smile which wanted to break her face in two.

'Gil. What a coincidence!'

'Well done.' He was smiling the smile she wanted to smile herself.

'How did you know?' she asked uncertainly.

He shrugged. 'I didn't. I saw it advertised and I just hoped. I've been loafing around this building for so long I was beginning to think that I'd get arrested for loitering.'

Eleanor was bewildered. 'But how did you know they'd offered it to me?'

'You should have seen yourself walking across the car park. You looked as if you'd grown a couple of inches overnight.' He stood back, his hands still on her shoulders, and surveyed her. 'You look great,' he said. 'More beautiful than ever.'

'Soft soap,' she muttered, still puzzled, but too overwhelmed with the pleasure of seeing him to be able to articulate her thoughts.

He bent to scratch the head of the pup. 'She is beautiful, isn't she, Jip?' he said to the dog, then glanced up at Eleanor, a wicked smile contorting his face.

'How did you know his name? And don't tell me that Gwen Jenkins has a sister running a sub-post office in Fulham because I shan't believe you.'

He laughed. 'You're not blushing,' he said, his eyes narrowing assessingly.

'No. But that doesn't answer my question.'

'I heard you calling him before you went in for the interview.'

'You mean you really have been hanging around all this time? Why?'

'I told you. I was hoping to see you. Why did you call him Jip?'

'I didn't. I called him Ben. But every time I opened my mouth to speak to him I found Jip's name coming out. In the end I gave in to my instincts and changed his name.'

Gil put out an arm and let it rest comfortably across the back of her neck. She let it be. His hand squeezed her shoulder. It was a glorious feeling. Free. She felt herself beginning to relax.

'Come back to Trenawr with me...'

That old certainty of his was still there, but she wasn't afraid of it any more. 'Yes. If you like.'

He grinned. 'My car's around the back...'

'I'll take mine, if you don't mind.'

He studied her for a while, then delved into his trouser pocket and produced a bunch of keys. He extracted a key from the ring and handed it to her. 'That's the key to my Land Rover. If you come back in my car and decide to change your mind you can drive the Land Rover back here to collect your own car.'

She looked at the key lying in her palm, and then at Gil. That expression was back on his face—the very last one she had seen before she left. And she hadn't been wrong. She wanted to cry out with delight.

'All right,' she conceded evenly.

She had wound her hair up into a knot for the interview. Once the open-topped car was spinning down the coast road she unpinned it and let it blow free. The roar of the engine and the rush of the clean salt air past her ears made conversation impossible. She was glad. She didn't want to talk. Every now and then she would look sideways at him and her heart would leap with happiness. Gil. Gil. Would it be all right? Probably not, but this time, at least, she was prepared to give it a try. To taste freedom.

She might have changed, but he hadn't. He was pleased to see her. More than that—he felt something; she was sure of it. And yet the man who always thought the worst of her was still packaged in that taut frame, behind those glinting eyes. He had obviously wanted to see her again. But the next time she did something . . . said something slightly off the mark, would he immediately jump to the wrong conclusion again? There was only one way to find out.

As they walked across the yard she asked, 'I still don't understand how you found out about the job.'

'I told you. I saw it advertised.'

'Do you usually read the job ads in *The Times Higher Educational Supplement*?'

'No. But I knew this job was coming up.'

Her stomach lurched queasily. 'Oh. Exactly how did you come by that knowledge?'

He opened the kitchen door. Old Jip came out and sniffed at the new Jip. The dogs grinned identical grins and then lolloped off together to stretch their legs.

'I've a good friend who works at the Alternative World Technology Institute. He came to dinner one night. We ended up talking about this and that. He was complaining about the shortage of funds for research into their projects. I offered to put up some money.'

'You mean . . .' She swallowed against the dryness of her mouth. 'You mean they were already planning to develop a soil erosion project? But they didn't have the cash?'

He shrugged. 'I don't know. He didn't mention specific projects. Though I told him all about your ideas. He was very impressed. He felt you'd got a completely new angle on the whole business.'

As they sauntered into the big, familiar kitchen Eleanor's heart was in her high-heeled, patent-leather court shoes. 'In other words you bought me my job.' Her voice was strained and small with hurt.

He frowned. 'No. I'll admit I could have done. I could quite easily have stipulated how the money was to be spent. But I trust those boffins at the Institute. They had complete control. I wasn't even consulted after a certain stage.'

'But you stated a preference?'

'No. Not even that. In fact, until I looked up the job ad I didn't even know that the soil had won. There were a lot of other ideas—alternative energy sources and so on—which were prime contenders.'

Eleanor sighed. 'Oh, well. Never mind. I'll telephone them later and tell them to get in touch with the other candidates.'

'What are you on about, Eleanor?'

She didn't want the job any more. Not since he had quite clearly wangled it for her, no matter what he said. He was a Machiavellian of a very high order. Once she had dissected his words she was sure she would be able to identify the omissions, the half-truths, which would reveal exactly how he had ensured that she was given the job, despite his protestations of innocence. It was a bitter disappointment, but she would weather it. There would be other jobs—not so exciting, of course, but at least won on her own merits. And, at any rate, the whole exercise had brought Gil and herself together again, so she could hardly complain. She had known from the start what he was like, and had concluded long ago that it would have been better to try to learn to live with his faults—as she had once claimed she was prepared to do with Edward's—than to lose him altogether.

She offered him a smile. 'What else has been happening in Trenawr these past couple of months? How are Gwen Jenkins and the Prossers and everybody?'

Gil looked at her suspiciously, then cupped his hands over his face and rubbed at his forehead with his fingertips, pressing hard. 'Eleanor. You don't believe me, do you?'

She took a few steps towards him, and tentatively reached out a hand to touch his shoulder. She smiled again. 'I really have learned a lot these past months,' she said softly. 'I'm afraid I'm not so easy to tease any more. But it doesn't matter. Really.' She inched closer, looking steadfastly up at him, waiting—hungrily now that she was near enough to breathe in the scent of him— for his mouth to close on hers, and the kiss to begin.

He stepped backwards. His eyes caught fire. 'I didn't set up the job for you, damn it,' he said harshly. 'I would have liked to, and I'll admit that I was delighted when I read the advertisement and knew you would be certain to apply. But I damn well didn't fix it, and you'd better believe it.'

Eleanor shrugged, edging closer again. 'Gil, really, it's neither here nor there. You like getting your own way. You like people to dance to your tune. But I don't *mind* any more. Don't you see?' And she laid the palms of her hands flat against his chest.

'You want to make love with me, don't you, Eleanor?' His voice was curt, accusing almost.

She was taken aback. 'I…well…that is…' She sighed. 'Yes. If you want the truth, I suppose I do.'

He wandered over to the fridge, took out a bottle of champagne, rejected it and then extracted a bottle of cold *vin du table*. He fetched two wine glasses at an equally leisurely pace and set them on the table. Then he crossed the kitchen to find the corkscrew, sat down in one of the wheel-backed chairs and began, very slowly, to open the bottle.

The glasses filled, he pushed one across the table towards her, then leaned back in his chair and sipped at his own. Eleanor felt distinctly uncomfortable. This rejection was the last thing she had expected.

'Sit down,' he said quietly, nodding at the chair opposite.

She slid into the seat.

'Are you still a virgin?' he asked coldly.

'I...' She met his eyes. 'Why do you ask?'

'Are you?'

'Yes. But I really don't see——'

'Good. Then drink that wine.'

'Why are you so angry with me?'

He bit the end of his thumb before replying, then looked hard into her eyes and said candidly, 'Because you've changed. And I don't think I like the new you.'

'What exactly do you object to?'

He shrugged. 'You don't blush any more. You're practically inviting yourself into my bed...'

'Well, of all the cheek!' Mortification swept through her. 'In June you did nothing but tell me I should change! And now you've got the nerve to... to... complain because I have!'

There was a taunting edge to his voice. 'I didn't mean you to change into a——'

He stopped himself. But she knew exactly what he'd been going to say. And all because *she'd* wanted *him* to kiss her. She put her hand into the pocket of her cream linen jacket and extracted the key to his Land Rover. Then she pushed the glass away. 'I don't drink and drive,' she said icily, getting to her feet.

'Sit down,' he ordered, glowering from under his darkly knitted brows. 'We've stormed out on misunderstanding after misunderstanding. Don't you think it's time we stayed put for once until we're absolutely, positively certain that we dislike each other?'

'I'm quite certain that I dislike you. And I couldn't care less about how you feel. Yet again you have chosen to think the worst of me. I had this stupid notion that I could live with your nasty mind. That I could make it not matter. But I can't.' She started towards the door.

'Sit down!' he roared.

'No.' She actually opened the door and walked through it.

His voice came through the doorway at such a volume that she actually felt the vibrations shaking her.

'Damn you, Eleanor! So you haven't changed that much after all, have you? You're just as hot-headed. Now come back here at once.'

She hesitated.

His voice when it came again was just as loud, but there was a strangulated note of restraint holding it in check. 'I am purposely not grabbing hold of you and making you come back and listen to me. I am giving you a free choice. I am trying to mend my ways. But if you don't do as I say I'm afraid I shall have to revert to my former self and put you in that seat by force! I let you go free once, but I don't think I can bear to do it again. It goes against the grain.'

She covered her mouth to hide a smile. They seemed to be wandering back into very familiar territory. She felt safe. And she couldn't help liking the things he was saying. She came back into the kitchen and sat down.

'Let me,' he said, propping his elbows on the table and leaning towards her, 'emphasise that I did not arrange for you to get that job. I let you go back to London on your little ownsome because I suddenly realised that until you had sorted out that mess of a life of yours all

by yourself you were going to be of no use to me at all—
that I was going to have to wait until you were ready
whether I liked it or not. Even I could see that fixing a
job for you was not going to advance my cause.'

'Well, I've sorted out my life. I am ready. And, to be
frank, I came here with you today with the highest ex-
pectations of being . . . used by you,' she retorted hotly.
'So where's the problem?'

'You once found the idea of being made love to by
me without the benefit of a diamond ring very
objectionable.'

'I once found a lot of things very objectionable. Like
the fact that you and Sylvia were lovers.'

'Lovers? You think that, and yet you still want come
into my bed? You see . . . You *have* changed for the
worse!'

'Stop making excuses, Gil. You and I both know that
Sylvia has nothing at all to do with your getting mad at
me. You're furious because I won't believe you about
the job. You want to protest your innocence to me, and
all I want to do is kiss you. I don't actually *care* whether
you're deceiving me or not, and you don't like it.'

'Of course I don't like it!'

'So don't blame Sylvia.'

'So Sylvia's role in my life doesn't bother you at all?'

'Of course it doesn't.'

'Humph.' Gil folded his arms and scowled. 'It might
interest you to know that Sylvia is a married woman
with two children. That she's a director in my company,
and that our relationship is, and always has been, strictly
of a business nature.'

'None of that interests me particularly.'

Gil glared at her. 'Look, I know all those clothes were
in the spare room, but they were only there because we'd

had some colleagues here for a slap-up meal and she knew she'd be drinking and she didn't want to drive herself home. As it happens someone gave her a lift— she just hadn't got round to collecting the clothes. That's all. She didn't even stay here the one night!'

'You'll be trying to tell me that you're a virgin next, Gil...' said Eleanor, absolutely straight-faced.

'I...' And then Gil gave a wry smile of recognition. 'Hoist,' he muttered, 'by my own petard... You're teasing me, aren't you?'

Eleanor said nothing.

'Look,' he continued, 'Sylvia's been working——'

'Don't bother to explain. Gwen Jenkins, bless her heart, put me straight on that score about ten minutes before I left Trenawr. She explained that your firm had bought out Sylvia's family's marine engineering company and that she was hoping to become a full business partner some day. Which, because of the nature of the take-over, she felt she had a right to expect. You must forgive my mistake. I was judging the woman by her taste in underwear.'

'Then you have the advantage of me. I have no notion of what her taste in underwear might be.'

'I realised that a long time ago.'

'Then why the hell didn't you come back?'

'Because Sylvia wasn't the only problem. You went to quite a lot of trouble to point out to me that I resembled a cuckoo in certain respects. How long had Mrs Williams been keeping that meal warm while you waited for those chicks to fly?'

He laughed then. 'Serendipity,' he said. 'Honestly. The analogy only came to mind as I was leaving the house to fetch you. That was when I saw the first chick stick its head out of the hole. I have to admit to thinking it was a rather clever comparison, though.'

'It was offensive. I still find it offensive. However, as luck would have it, events later conspired to make me very grateful for the ornithology lesson. I found a flat as soon as I got back to London. For two weeks I tried ringing my parents daily or calling back home to re-assure them that I was all right. They fussed dreadfully. Then I decided to metaphorically emigrate to Africa. I told them not to ring. I was too busy. That I'd be in touch in a fortnight's time—not sooner. When I finally called round they were out. They'd joined an evening class in calligraphy. They are more than happy without me, it seems. Now that the cuckoo has finally flown they are back to doing what comes naturally—to them at any rate.'

Gil chuckled. 'Drink some more of that wine,' he smiled. 'And tell me what's happened to Porky.'

'Edward married his secretary last week. I'm afraid it was a rather hasty affair. He let his standards slip, apparently, and there's a little piglet due about seven and a half months from now. However, you will be de-lighted to hear that they are blissfully happy, and western civilisation has yet to come crashing down around their ears.'

His laughter, this time, was more robust. 'So your life is all in apple-pie order.'

'Not quite. But about as good as I'm likely to get, I suppose. Why aren't you drinking your wine?'

'You were trying to seduce me not long ago. I decided I'd rather keep a clear head.'

'I wasn't planning to seduce you. I'd rather hoped that there'd be no need. It seems I was wrong.'

His teeth flashed white as he smiled broadly. 'Tell me that you'll keep the job, and I'll kiss you immediately.'

'Only kiss me?'

'No. But that's where I'll start.'

She sighed. 'I'm only going to agree to take the job when I'm convinced that I got it on my own merits.'

His face tightened into lines of annoyance. 'Why don't you believe me?' That fire was back in his voice, the intensity in his eyes.

'Why should I? You're quite capable of rigging it, and lying about it, too.'

'Lying? For crying out——'

'It's horrible, isn't it, being accused of lying? But you have to admit that it does seem a natural conclusion for me to draw. After all, it would be too much of a co-incidence for that job just to happen along...'

'I've already told you——'

'It's not very nice having someone jump to unpleasant conclusions about you, is it? And in case you think I'm turning the tables on you—teasing *you* for a change, then let me put you straight. I'm not. I honestly think you must have rigged the job.'

He ran one hand raspingly over his chin. Then he stood up, paced impatiently across to the fridge, took out the champagne, reached down two flutes from the dresser, strode across to where she was sitting and caught hold of her hand in a very perfunctory manner. He pulled her to her feet.

'Come on,' he said brusquely.

'Where?'

'Upstairs.'

Eleanor followed him silently as he marched upstairs and into his bedroom. She began to feel a bit nervous. Well, very nervous actually. She had come to this house hoping that they would make love. She had known that it would be a loveless activity, on his part at least. But she had expected it to be passionate, none the less. Very, very passionate. This was anything but.

He slammed the bottle and glasses on to the walnut chest of drawers.

'Get on the bed,' he ordered tersely.

'But I... The thing is...'

'Shut up and do as I say.'

She surveyed him suspiciously. He didn't look like a man with sex on his mind. Anything but, actually. Anxiously she perched on the edge of the bed. She really didn't know whether to be pleased or disappointed. This was all very disturbing, but, oddly, she didn't feel threatened.

'Not like that,' he muttered exasperatedly. 'Lie on it properly. Put your head on the pillows.'

'What is going on, Gil?'

'Wait and see.'

She began to ease off her shoes.

'You don't need to bother with that. You can keep your shoes on.'

Pulling a bewildered face, she heaved herself into the middle of the bed, and lay back, looking at her shoes winking at her from afar.

He picked up the phone and dialed. At last he was connected. 'Hi, Richard? It's Gil.'

He came to lie beside her on the bed, putting the receiver between them, so that Eleanor could hear.

'Gil! How are you? We finally spent your money today. I was going to ring later and let you know,' Richard replied.

'Good. How did things go?'

'Tremendous. We had a marvellous response—excellent candidates. It was quite a job shortlisting them. In the end there was no contest. A University of London girl—really knows her stuff. Very original mind. Brilliant.'

'Uh-huh. What's the research going to be?'

'Oh, I should have called you weeks back and let you know. We had quite a fight over that one. There was a big contingent wanting to get some research under way on chemical energy sources. But I felt our lab resources weren't up to it. In the end I'm afraid I cribbed those ideas you were telling me about—you know, on soil erosion. That friend of yours, whoever he is, really provided me with food for thought. There are research avenues there which I really feel need pursuing, and the woman we've appointed will be more than able to——'

'Richard? Sorry to interrupt—can I call you back? Something's just cropped up...'

The phone was replaced on the chest of drawers.

Gil looked coolly at her. 'It's nice to see you blushing so prettily again, Eleanor. I thought you might have forgotten how it's done.'

'I...OK. I'm sorry. I believe you now.'

He smiled at her, stretching out beside her on the bed.

'Gil, why are we lying here in our clothes?'

He turned his head sideways and looked at the bottle and glasses.

'I'm ready to be seduced now,' he said, his eyes glittering russet and green. 'Why don't you open the champagne and see if you can get me tipsy?'

'I... This is all back to front!' Her face had suddenly flamed scarlet, and she felt quite tongue-tied.

'Go on,' he taunted, a mocking smile playing around his lips. 'Open the bottle.' And he stretched his arms languidly above his head, waiting.

Oh, damn him. He was doing it again. Crossly she sat up and reached across him for the bottle. She started to untwist the wire cage, screwing up her eyes and holding the bottle at arm's length.

'Hurry up.'

'Oh, shut up!' She positioned her thumbs ready, to ease out the cork, tucking her cheek against one shoulder as she did so, and closing her eyes tight.

'Get a move on!'

'I'm doing my best... The cork seems to be a bit stuck.'

'You're not pushing, that's all.'

'I am!'

'You're not! You're scared!'

She screwed her eyes tighter shut and pushed a little harder against the cork. 'I'm not scared!' she muttered defiantly.

'For goodness' sake, Eleanor! You think absolutely nothing of dangling over the edge of a cliff on a piece of glorified string, but you're frightened to pop a champagne cork. You really are the most contradictory person I've ever met in my life!'

'I'm not! It's just that——'

He sat up and laughed, shaking and quaking with mirth. Then he put one arm around her shoulder, and with the other hand reached out and took the bottle and flicked the cork with his thumb. It popped loudly and obligingly, and fizzed gloriously as he hastily grabbed the glasses and filled them.

'You are wonderful!' he murmured, slurping the overspill of froth from his glass. 'I couldn't believe it when you came across as such a cool madam—such a

self-possessed woman of the world! And then I realised
what had really changed. You've got the hang of proper
conversation at last! Your mind and your mouth are
working as a team these days. I'm sorry I was so slow
on the uptake. I promise I shall never dare think the
worst of you again!'

She couldn't help smiling, too. Well, more than
smiling, really, because laughter, accompanied by champagne, was heady stuff. And then he hugged her and
said, 'Tell me you love me.'

'I... Honestly! What a cheek! What on earth makes
you think that I love you?'

'You called your dog Jip.'

'So did you!'

'Ah, yes. Then I must love you too... it's the only
explanation. You'll have to marry me now!'

Her eyes opened wide with astonished delight. Was
he teasing again? How on earth could she find out? But
she didn't have a chance to enquire because he began to
kiss her. It was a very delicate kiss. It was hardly a kiss
at all really, just the breathy meeting of lips, at first.
And then a sort of nibbling and biting, and then his
mouth opened warm upon hers and they were kissing
properly.

Somewhere in the tangle of arms and shoes and clothes
he managed to relieve her of her glass. But he didn't
stop kissing her. She was faintly conscious of his fingers
picking neatly at the buttons on her blouse. But most
of all she was conscious of desire, hot and desperate,
surging through her veins.

He was kissing her with a gleeful urgency, his tongue
exploring rapaciously while she opened to him. Her own
hands travelled down his back, feeling the broad planes
of muscles and bone beneath the cotton of his shirt.

Wantonly, they lingered on the curve of his hard buttocks, pulling him infinitesimally closer to her as she
moved sensuously against him. His hand came round to
cup her breast, heavy in his large hand. His fingers
stroked against the lace and silk of her underwear,
finding her nipple, and letting his palm brush lightly
across it time and again.

The pleasure leapt in her throat, so that she set free
a sharp moan of delight. He took his mouth from hers,
then, and ran the tip of his tongue softly against her
cheek. She kissed him in return—little, sucking, papery
kisses against his barbed chin, her eyes closed, her mind
lost in the power of instinct. He turned his mouth along
the line of her jaw, down across her throat, while her
hands clutched and rumpled at the thick, strong hair of
his head. She spread her fingers sumptuously among its
dense waves, finding the duck's tail at the nape of his
neck and fingering it tenderly.

His mouth settled in the dip between her breasts,
tracing the hollows of flesh and bone, and making her
shudder helplessly with yearning. His teeth caught the
lace edge of her bra and drew it back, so that the demanding swell of her breasts pressed closer to his face.
With hungry fingers he unfastened the centre clasp, and
pulled back the fine white lace. Now her breasts, creamy
white and full, spilled out into the warmth of his breath.
Her nipples stood in proud, rosy peaks which thrust
willingly against his cupped hand, thrilling to the slow,
circular caress of his thumb.

Her legs shook a little as he moulded her breasts beneath his demanding fingers. Her nipples were extraordinarily sensitive, alive with pleasurable excitement,
and sending darts of urgent desire to that deep, moist

place that waited, like a half-open rosebud, to enfold him in its velvety depths.

And then he drew back and knelt over her, his breath jerky, his chest expanding and contracting unevenly as he looked down into her face. He smiled a sensual half-smile, his eyes gleaming soft and dark beneath hooded lids, as little by little he undressed her, letting his eyes linger on every inch of her flesh that he revealed. She didn't once let her hands leave him, reaching out her arms as he peeled away her stockings, to let her fingers trail against the small of his back. Her whole body called out to him. At last he straddled her, clad only in a pair of black briefs.

She drank in the sight of his powerful shoulders, his broad, silken chest, golden-brown and scattered with hairs. She let her eyes run downwards, remembering from the summer days the dark hairs below his navel, converging on the mid-line, disappearing beneath the narrow band of cloth. She spread her fingers against his skin, then dug them hard against the packed muscle beneath.

A soft moan of pleasure stirred in his throat, and he dipped his head to nuzzle his lips against her breasts, drawing from her fresh pangs of aching desire. The cool sheet beneath her shoulders contrasted with the burning heat of her breasts. She gasped with delight at the exquisite pleasure of his mouth as they drew her thrumming nipples deep into his mouth, caressing them with his tongue.

When she felt that desire must choke her, when instinct was pounding her flesh against his, arching and aching, bone against bone, he at last let his fingers trail across the fine skin on the inside of her thigh, sending great charges of molten pleasure cascading through her.

He discarded the last barrier then, revealing his proud glorious manhood, rooted hard, waiting. She turned towards him, her eyes misted, willing him to take her for his own.

There was a pause, a moment, while he hung above her, looking deep into her eyes. Somewhere her voice was sobbing out to him. She saw him smile, before his flesh came close against her face and eyes, blinding her to everything except the raw, crying need of her blood, answered at last by his body as, rose-petal soft, she opened and enfolded him. Deep inside her he thrust hard, male, powered by a need as forceful as her own, shudderingly taut beneath her splayed hands, groaning out his desire. Shock and delight carried her with him, surging and pressing, clamouring and pushing until with a wild, abandoned cry she clenched around him, her senses whirling into a shapeless, dark, convulsive ecstasy.

Replete, whole at last, drenched in sweat and sweet happiness, they lay silent for a long time. At last he raised a lazy finger and ran it from the bridge of her nose to the tip.

'That,' he murmured, 'was very precious, my love. A homecoming indeed ...'

She turned her shining eyes to him and smiled. 'Oh, Gil ...' she sighed, too happy to make words form on her lips.

Wrapped together, they dozed, until he kissed her again, and reached for the champagne glasses.

'The fizz has gone,' he smiled. 'Let's refresh it.' And he poured a little more of the effervescent wine into their glasses before making love to her once again, slowly, lazily, thoroughly and delightfully.

Beyond the window a smoky, dusky haze settled. The two Jips scratched and scrabbled at the kitchen door but Gil and Eleanor did not hear them. Their world had shrunk to the size of each other's eyes.

'Tell me about yourself, Gil...' murmured Eleanor at last.

'What do you want to know?'

She shrugged. 'Everything, I suppose. What sort of porridge your mother makes—you know, important stuff like that.'

He let out a soft laugh. But he didn't say anything.

She pressed her cheek against his chest. 'Did you really mean it, Gil, when you sort of said you loved me? Or was it...you know...were you teasing?'

'I was never more serious in my life,' he said gravely. Then he propped himself up on one elbow and looked down on her. 'Why do you need to ask me that?'

She sighed. 'Oh. Because, well, back in the summer you seemed to despise me so much of the time.'

He was silent for a while. A very long while. He looked at her all the time, though, his eyes a muted hazel. Then he said, 'There were four chicks in my nest, all jostling for porridge, Eleanor. I was the eldest. Then came Hilary—she's a bit of a pain—she was born to shop, and Alison—who was, I'm sorry to say, born to nag—but very kind with it. And then Suzanne. She was the youngest. She was very sweet. That pink room, where you slept...she chose the decorations for that... It's like her, the room. Pretty. Sweet. Summery. Everyone loved Suzanne.' He swallowed hard. 'She, sadly, was born to die. She had leukaemia...' He paused again, and when he spoke next his voice was thick with emotion. 'She was very brave and always very happy. She loved life. But she died when she was only fifteen. I watched her fade and I was powerless to stop it.'

Eleanor put her hand to her mouth. She could feel the pain bleeding from his words. 'I'm sorry,' she whispered, aching for him deep within her heart.

'I loved Suzanne. I've had plenty of women friends, Eleanor. Plenty. But I've never been in love with any of them. And then one day someone young and lovely and full of life walked into the village and my heart turned over. I fell in love with her image, and I had great hopes of falling in love with the reality, too. I plied Gwen Jenkins with questions and I booked a table for dinner, and then I came down on the beach to ask you to come out with me—despite that awful ring you wore. I looked for you on the sand, but you weren't there. And then I saw you in the sea. And you were drowning. You were dying in front of my eyes. And I thanked God that this time I had the power to intervene.' He stopped.

'Don't say any more,' murmured Eleanor huskily. 'I understand.'

'Do you?' He laid his head on her breast. 'I hope so. I half loved you, half hated you. You seemed so careless of your life...oh, not just because you wouldn't accept how close you'd come to losing it, but because you seemed to be squandering its joys. Every time you did something life-affirming—like letting Porky trot off—my heart would leap with hope. And then you'd do something crazy to spoil it. Or, at least, that was how it seemed.'

He sighed. 'And then you saved Jip's life, and I knew I'd got you badly wrong. Deep down you loved life, Eleanor. And I knew I loved you, too.'

'Oh...' She bit her lip, remembering lying with him on the wet grass, trembling in his arms. She recalled the smell of his shirt, soft against her cheek. 'I thought...well, I knew you must have come to trust me to have gone over the edge yourself. But I still thought you despised me. I hated myself for... for loving you. Because it made a fool of me.' She ran her tongue across her lips. 'But I couldn't stop loving you. So I had to face up to the fact that I really had been a fool—for years and years. If I loved you—which I did—then I had to accept that I'd been wrong. It took me a long time to work it out. It was like fitting a jigsaw together, very slowly and very painfully.

'When I was down on that ledge with Jip I was worried that anything I might do to entice him into the bag might make him behave unpredictably and dangerously. Because I didn't understand dogs, and so I couldn't seem to trust my instincts with him. That was how it was between my parents and me. We could never understand each other properly. They were frightened for me because they couldn't comprehend me. I was always unpredictable to them. And try as I might I could never be like them.'

She drifted for a while on the silence between them. Then she said, 'You set me free, Gil. I've spread my wings now. I've flown. And right now I feel as if I've touched the sky.'

'Do you really love me?'

She couldn't answer that. There was no word bigger than yes, and it was too small a word to tell what she felt in her heart. Instead she closed her eyes and let her mouth drift—instinctively—into a smile. Which he covered, gently, gratefully, with a kiss.

A program of collections of three complete novels by the most-requested authors with the most-requested themes. Be sure to look for one volume each month with three complete novels by top-name authors.

In September: **BAD BOYS**

Dixie Browning
Ann Major
Ginna Gray

No heart is safe when these hot-blooded hunks are in town!

In October: **DREAMSCAPE**

Jayne Ann Krentz
Anne Stuart
Bobby Hutchinson

Something's happening! But is it love or magic?

In December: **SOLUTION: MARRIAGE**

Debbie Macomber
Annette Broadrick
Heather Graham Pozzessere

Marriages in name only have a way of leading to love....

Available at your favorite retail outlet.

REQ-G2

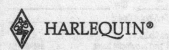 HARLEQUIN®

 Silhouette

Relive the romance...
Harlequin® is proud to bring you

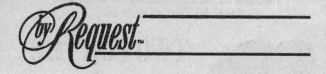

A new collection of three complete novels every month. By the most requested authors, featuring the most requested themes.

Available in January:

They're ranchers, horse trainers, cowboys...
They're willing to risk their lives.
But are they willing to risk their hearts?

Three complete novels in one special collection:

RISKY PLEASURE by JoAnn Ross
VOWS OF THE HEART by Susan Fox
BY SPECIAL REQUEST by Barbara Kaye

Available wherever Harlequin books are sold.